The Blue Moon Catastrophe

Justin Bauer

Edited by Daniel Killinger
Cover design by Josh Bennett

For Cody

ACKNOWLEDGMENTS

I'd like to thank Daniel Killinger for his encouragement
after reading and editing my early drafts. You inspire me to
be a better writer and storyteller.
I would also like to thank Josh Bennett for his enthusiasm.
It has been a pleasure working with you on the cover and I
hope to do it again in the near future.
I would also like to show my gratitude towards my parents
and Lydia. You have been supportive of my endeavors,
even when they have been less than deserving.
I guess all of this wouldn't be possible without my time in
the hospitality industry, for which I am eternally jaded.

"I was born with the devil in me. I could not help the fact that I was a murderer, no more than a poet can help the inspiration to sing..."

-H. H. Holmes

1

What was supposed to just be another day at work would trigger my omega. I was content right up until the aging room phone provided the rudest kind of awakening; the piercing shrill of the ringer viciously tore me from sleep. My first instinct was to feel anger with the intruding noise and possibly destroy the source, but that was all quickly followed by my sense of duty. Rolling to my right, I answered the phone that rested next to a dirty glass on a wooden nightstand that was embedded into the drywall. I decided to keep my eyes closed, if only to deny that I was needed to at least answer some work related question. Time stands still when your heart beats to a routine.

"Hello," I said into the receiver; the cheaply made plastic was cool to the touch.

"I wake you up?" Samantha asked. She already knew the answer as both of our tones gave it away.

"Yeah, no big deal. What's going on?" I asked as I finally opened my eyes to the dark bedroom.

"I don't have anyone to check the due outs, and that was supposed to happen two hours ago. I figured I'd let you sleep in for a while but I need 'em checked in case anybody's holding up."

"Okay, I'll be down in a moment," I said as neutrally as I could fake. It had been a long couple of days at the property as I had pulled a last minute night audit shift after covering the previous morning on the desk. Too tired to care at that point, my eyes adjusted to the dimly lit hotel room as I checked the dusty alarm clock to see that it was, in fact, two o'clock in the afternoon. At least this wasn't an emergency.

"Thanks," Samantha said before I hear the click of her ending the call.

Hanging up the receiver, I stretched before sitting up in the king size bed. I was absorbed into the chill of the room as I tossed the linen from my body. Rubbing my eyes, I wanted to deny the day, unplug the phone, and let the hotel float without me for a bit longer. But it was a Sunday, and without a head housekeeper on duty, it was up to me. Standing up, I stretched again and reached for the ceiling as my body began to accept the fact that it was no longer at rest. My joints would ache in spite of this. Coffee suddenly became more than a desire as my body clock demanded the caffeine in the form of an acute headache. I left the bedroom and went to the kitchen where I started to brew a pot of my sweet, sweet addiction before entering the living area where the company had given me my own work computer with access to all of the current property data, as well as an Onity key programmer. Given the choice to work in my apartment or in the main office, I pick isolation every time that it's simply routine work. Bringing the desktop PC out of hibernation, I printed off the list of guests that were due to check out. With thirteen rooms in total to inspect, I programmed a housekeeping key for myself so that I could enter the rooms. I quickly put on some kind of business attire that reflects my position but doesn't show that I care all that much, a pair of black pants and a light blue dress shirt that I also typically wear when working the desk. Once clothed, I pocketed my old flip phone, poured myself a cup of black coffee into my favorite Ohio State mug and left my apartment unit that was on the fourth story. The solid wooden door was unlike any other on the property, as it wasn't a standard room at the hotel. It exited straight to a concrete stairwell that included another locked door to the public stairwell on the third floor. My room was the only unit on the fourth story. It spanned a solid half of the floor space of the property, had a functional kitchen, bathroom, living space, bedroom, closet, and storage area. The living area contained the perk of having a sliding glass door that allowed one to walk out onto the flat part of the roof where I kept a small garden that had been retired for the year as the weather had just brought in the season's first frost.

My name is Jessie Wilson, and I was an assistant manager at the Blue Moon Inn on the northern outskirts of town. With safety and security being the highest priority, I'll admit that I wouldn't want this same job in different parts of the city. And yet this place experiences its own evil from time to time. This job has changed the way that I interact with people. I feel myself becoming apathetic. Often when dealing with scum, I feel myself unable to relate. This job has changed me in a way that has brought on this confession that will be delivered in full over the course of our meetings.

To this point, I still wasn't sure whether or not I was comfortable living on the property. I had been living there for the previous seven months since my promotion. Residing in my place of employment is somehow reminiscent of the deepest layers of Hell; and yet it was rent free, carried the additional perk of no longer making the daily commute to and from the pit, and corporate had authorized a nice pay increase in the case of making myself so available. All of this was encouraged by my boss and property manager, Adam McCline, as it enabled him to mentally check out as he started coming to the place less and less. I really liked him as a person, but he was a lousy boss as his home troubles seemed to be spelling out the approaching end of his marriage. He used that burden to fuel a drinking habit while I held down the fort more often than not.

The stairwell carried the stale odor of smoke with a hint of mildew. The building was old and in desperate need of a remodel. With flat screen televisions and hard wood floors becoming a brand standard, our property was the black sheep as we were left with these old bulky televisions from the nineties as well as carpet from the same time period. Red stains on the carpet were often confused for blood, and it became a favorite scenario of mine to inform the guests that blood does not hold a deep red color as it dries, but a crusted brown. The fact that I know this usually puts them off a bit, but wine is thinner and less offensive than blood.

I entered the dimly lit hallway of the third floor. The texture of carpet beneath my shoes was a contrast to the concrete of the stairwell that always made me nervous as the feeling represented the divide between self exile and the workplace. The smell of stale smoke was more prominent here as this was the designated smoking floor. The heavy door to the stairwell closed hard behind me as I found myself in the middle of the hallway that stretched out in what seemed like an infinite and uniform tunnel. The aging drywall that lined the corridor had yellowed with increasing depth the closer it got to the ceiling. I had three rooms to check on this floor. I turned to my left, towards the lower numbers to check room 310 that was left open by a Jason Thompson. I still knocked before vocalizing my presence. When I received no response, I entered the room to find that Mr. Thompson had left opting not to check out at the desk. He also had what appeared to be a good time as bottles from a twelve pack of beer and three empty cans of energy drinks were scattered about the room. He left every single light in the room turned on, as well as the television. I turned everything off before moving forward.

Room 317 didn't leave the door open, but it was much the same in that they were gone and had left the odor of beer that defined the aftermath of weekends on the smoking floor. I simply marked, 'c/o' next to the room number on the due out list, and moved on.

The final room on the third floor that needed to be checked was 329. As I approached the room, I could hear voices coming from the other side of the door. At least two people, a man and a woman. Possibly a second man, but I wasn't sure. The name on the list was Penelope Rice. She had left the Do Not Disturb sign inserted into the key slot. Figuring I'd try to avoid face contact before knocking, I went back to 317, sat down and called them from the phone in that room.

It rang four times before Penelope answered. It was another four seconds of awkward shuffling noises before she spoke aggressively with a demanding, "What?"

"This is Jessie with management, and I'm sorry to bother you," I started, "but checkout was two hours ago. At this time we ask that you either check out, or if you're looking to stay over we'll need a method of payment at the front desk."

"Oh, are we late?" Penelope asked. She sounded tired and strung out as she said, "I'm sorry, I'll be right down to pay for another night."

"Thank you," I said to a dead line. She had explained herself and hung up on me before I could respond. I figured I'd check the rest of the rooms that were due out, and then check with the front desk to let Samantha know that 329 should be down to pay.

Penelope and her company were trouble, but thus far they've kept to themselves and have typically paid on time. I wasn't sure what they were up to, and without that evidence there was no choice but to allow them to stay over as long as they paid. They had all of the traits of bad guests in that they paid in cash day to day, refused housekeeping service for the five days they've already been here, not to mention Penelope is the only one I've seen and she's got a damaged looking, hard drug face. Caking on the makeup, she can't layer enough to cover the look that cries out, 'I actually am this hopeless!' These kind of people simply came with the job, and after four years, I can't say that this sort of thing bothers or surprises me in any way shape or form.

I went back to the stairwell which was directly adjacent to room 317. As I passed around the one hundred and eighty degree turn at the second floor I fantasized about replacing the dead air conditioning unit to help the stairwell breathe. Fading red brick walls lined the stairwell, and cracks running through the structure told of things these walls have witnessed: domestic abuse and drunken tirades that resulted in people's falling here; burn marks where cigarettes had been put out were scattered on the grey concrete stairs, as were the butts themselves that lay in the thin layers of their own ashes. There was also a fair share of coffee stains from my cup splashing over as I often took to the stairs faster than I should.

The second floor also carried a faint smell of stale cigarette smoke, but it was less apparent on the nonsmoking floor. It was impossible to keep guests from smoking as our property did accept cash payment without a credit card and did not punish those who had offended the policy. I had heard that with respectable chains there are up to five hundred dollar penalties that are nonnegotiable. That kind of policy made up my dreams, as nonsmoking rooms smelling of smoke was one of the most common complaints we'd get.

Luckily for me, the nine rooms on second floor had been vacated. During the time it took to knock on each door and inspect them all individually, I had finished my coffee. With twelve of the thirteen rooms checked, all that was left was room 113 on the ground floor. Taking a moment to look at the empty mug, I decided it would be wise to head back to my apartment and get a refill before checking the last room and possibly getting stuck at the front desk. While I do enjoy my coffee black, the acidity of it dictated that I put just a bit of milk and sugar into my second cup.

This particular Blue Moon Inn was

unique in that it wasn't built to the brand standard specifics. This property had originally flown under a different banner but was later bought out, remodeled, and simply conformed to meet the standards associated with the Blue Moon logo. While the second and third floors both confined the guests to interior entry, the ground floor rooms had direct access to the parking lot in the manner to which motels were accustomed. This meant stepping out into the crisp fall air to check the final room on the list of due outs.

Upon exiting the stairwell into the main lobby, Samantha emerged from the back office area to check on the sound I had made. Looking out, she wore a blue and black hijab which she rarely displayed anymore. She had married into Islam and only wore it on occasions when she wasn't at odds with her husband. Once she saw that I was not a guest, she set a romance novel to the counter, open and with the pages facing down to save her spot.

The main lobby was actually clean on this occasion. It was one big room that consisted of a waiting area which included four armchairs and two tall standing aluminum lamps that surrounded a long grey oval table, all on a dirty rug with years of stains that were begging for replacement. In the back left corner was the coffee bar which included coffee and tea, the closest thing we have to some kind of, 'breakfast.' The counter at the coffee bar had a light dusting of sugar and powdered creamer, and the canister labeled 'decaf' was stained with the splatter of coffee that had been too aggressively drawn. Someone had also abandoned a full cup of black coffee at the far left corner of the counter. Of the four canisters, there were two that contained regular coffee, one decaf, and one for hot water that was used for brewing tea. These canisters were in the middle of this counter, while to the left and right were these structures that held a number of Styrofoam cups, sugar, creamer canisters, stir sticks, teabags, and hot pink packets of artificial sweetener. Below the counter were three cupboards, two of which were used for storage, the third had a swinging slot and was labeled with a small white sign that read, "Trash." On the other side of the waiting area and coffee bar was the front desk which started at the wall by the main entrance, took a forty-five degree turn for two feet, and then a second forty-five degree turn where it went for another three and a half to four feet before ending into the wall. There was a single elevator, that I rarely used, which was a straight line from the main entrance. The doors to the elevator shared the same color as the walls in the lobby, which often resulted in multiple guests missing it. There was an opening in between the elevator and the main desk that entered a lengthy hallway. This part of the floor was typically the most neglected as stains a week old remained on it. There were three doors on the left in this hallway which led to the staff laundry room, a lost and found storage closet, and finally, the stairway at the end. On the right were two doors. The first was labeled with the words, "Employees Only" and entered the back area that contained a break room, a wretched restroom that was in desperate need of cleaning every twelve hours, and an office the size of a closet that opened up to the front desk area in the lobby. The second was a glass door that was always propped open. In there was a vending area that included two washers, three dryers, a soda machine, a vending machine, a laundry soap dispenser, and an ice machine; all of the essentials. Straight back at the end of the hall was a glass door that exited to the parking lot on the back side of the building.

"How's it goin'?" I asked as I walked toward the front desk. I took a drink from my coffee and sighed as I set the mug down to the counter.

"It's goin'. Pretty quiet now that it's past noon."

"Speaking of which," I started, "everyone upstairs other than 329 is gone. I'm gonna check 113 now, and I'll let you know."

"Awesome," Samantha stated as her line of vision shifted to the computer screen. She started mechanically checking out the rooms that were already gone before speaking again, "Should I call 329?"

"Yeah, give em a buzz if they're not down here by the end of your shift," I said calmly. "Either that or let me know and I'll harass them!"

"Sounds good," Samantha nodded.

Lifting my cup of coffee, I turned away from the desk and exited through the main entrance. It was a bit colder than I had expected, but it was a welcome change of pace from the previous summer. The record breaking heat and humidity equated to the kind of suffering I could live without. Turning to the left, 113 was the first room. As I approached, I noticed that the curtains were closed. I also noticed that the only car in the lot was parked in front of the door. It was a white four-door Chrysler Concord that had seen a couple of accidents. The driver's side door had been drilled by something recently, and the front windshield had a crack that webbed out from the passenger's side where the damage was centered. The model looked to be about ten to twelve years old and had Ohio plates that had expired back in January. I figured that the car had belonged to the guest, a Miss Emily Edwards, according to the list of due outs.

One of our inserts was sticking out of the key card slot and read, "Privacy Please." Being two hours after the checkout time, I would not respect the request. Knocking heavily upon the door, I intended to wake a guest that had possibly overslept. I waited for ten seconds before I knocked again and vocalized my presence, "Hello? Housekeeping!" Another ten seconds passed by and I heard no reaction from the other side of the door. At this point I was hoping that I was mistaken and that the car had belonged to somebody else. I pulled the housekeeping key card from my left side breast pocket and unlocked the room door. It inched open before it stopped abruptly due to the application of the security latch.

That's when I saw her through the inch and a half opening that the latch had allowed. She was lying on top of an untouched and properly made bed. It was the first time that I had ever found a dead body. She was fully clothed, on her back, and at first glance, I could tell that she wasn't breathing. Noise from the TV droned on with a high speed car chase from some action flick I've never seen. The sound of heavily compressed gunfire is now something that I still associate with finding her, as it has since brought her image to mind. Her eyes were these closed black craters that consisted of makeup and fatigue. She wore a white hooded sweatshirt, blue jeans, and hadn't even gotten to take off her pink Chuck Taylors. I stood in the cold and backed away when the heat of the room had seeped out to touch my face. The heat carried a terrible smell, and I felt sick as I recoiled and began to heave. The hum of the heater blared on as did the white noise in the background of the raging car chase. I gagged as though I would vomit but finally caught my breath and sighed heavily in order to catch my own balance. Her hair was dirty blonde and growing in brown at the roots, fried from at least a decade of coloring. Her face had been caked white. But the worst of it had to have been that her stomach protruded higher than the rest of her, and I could only assume that she was pregnant. From the distance, my first guess ended up being correct; overdose. A needle rested on the nightstand with some kind of polluted

leftover brown substance at the edge of the
barrel, a cooked spoon on top of the room
phone.

In an instant, I took all of this in.
Many seconds had passed before I realized
that my jaw was hanging open. It was a
moment after that when I came to the
realization that I had dropped my favorite
Ohio State mug to the concrete below;
Brutus' face was broken in half on top of the
wet ceramic remains. I swore under my
breath, shut the door to the room, and
backed away into the parking lot.

The cool air no longer played a
variable in that, once the heat of the room
had touched my face, I became
overwhelmingly hot. Breaking into a sweat, I
untucked my shirt and started to undo the
buttons. Once the shirt was open, I stood
there in the parking lot facing the Chrysler.
Opening my mouth, I could only make a
sound that expressed the panicked state in
which I had found myself, some contorted
and pathetic squeak that was cut short by
the choke of a quick breath. Closing my
eyes, I covered my face with my hands and
sighed heavily in a vain attempt to calm
myself.

I had always figured that this day
would come, but in the four moderately
quiet years that I had been employed here, I
came to ignore that possibility. Finding a
dead guest was the first new issue I've faced
in quite some time, and with the fresh
anxiety, an excitement was brought to my
heart that I could only interpret as shame. I
should be mechanical. I should be able to

simply go into the office, call the police, file an incident report with corporate, deal with the police, and be done with it. But when the day finally came and I had collected myself, my first action was to reach into my pocket and grab my cell phone with the intent to call my boss.

When Adam answered his phone he sounded casual in saying, "What do you want?"

"Guest in 113 is dead," I responded without hesitation.

"Please," he sighed heavily, "tell me you're lying." It was strange how calm he sounded.

"Wish that were the case man, but it's not. There's a body, and I can't get into the room without breaking the latch lock. From what I can see, there's a dirty needle on the nightstand. Looked pregnant."

"Were you the one to find her?" Adam asked.

"Yes," I quietly answered.

"Good! I'll be there in twenty minutes. And hey, Jessie, do me a favor,"

"Yeah, what is it?" I asked.

"You're on location; you make the call to the police. I should beat them there to help you deal with this."

"Will do, I'll make that call. Thanks, Adam."

"No problem, man, it's my job. I mean, you are management, but if you didn't call me or I didn't respond to a dead body report from my MOD, we'd be done. Out of jobs!" He paused for a moment before continuing, "You covered audit last night, didn't you?"

"Yes, I did. It's been a long couple of days, man," I stated coldly.

"I can imagine. Just chill out, make that phone call and I'll be there. Once we're done with the police, you can take off, alright?"

"Sounds like a plan."

"Good," Adam said with a sense of cool that escapes me still.

"Peace," I said to finish the conversation.

"Piss off!" Adam said before hanging up on me.

Shutting the phone as I lowered it from my ear, I waited only a second longer before noticing that the chill of the air had caught up with the moment, and I was freezing. I made a slight left turn back towards the main entrance and buttoned up my shirt as I went inside.

Samantha could see my concern as I walked around the desk and towards the employees only door, "Everything alright?"

"Not really," I said as I hooked through the door to the break room and went towards the office. As I passed the time clock I told her, "The woman in 113 is dead in there, and I can't get into the room because of the security latch! I'm gonna call the police and wait for Adam."

Samantha's eyes widened as she looked away from her romance novel, "Damn. Adam's on his way?"

"Yeah. I've already called him, and he said he should beat the police here to help me deal with this," I said in a way that expressed my fear.

"So you saw her? You sure she's dead?"

"As sure as I can be at that distance," I mechanically recited before pausing. I felt a sudden sense of pity for the dead junkie in the next room over, "She's not breathing, and by the look of it, she's been there for a while. How long has she been registered to the room?" I asked as I sat down in the back office chair.

"Otis checked her in on Friday. She paid for the two nights up front and asked for no service."

"The bed was made up as though she didn't sleep in it at all," I said bluntly.

"You think she's been dead since Friday night?" Samantha asked with a hint of excitement in her voice.

"More than likely," I sighed as I lifted the phone receiver in the office and called the nonemergency line of the Columbus Police Department.

Adam did beat the police to the scene by a solid hour and twenty minutes. He pulled into the parking lot in his dark blue Saturn with the broken passenger's side mirror. I think that the damage had been done more than a year prior to this incident. Adam sported a new haircut that was about an inch and a half of thick dark brown hair. He was dressed well in a recently ironed white button down shirt and a pair of crisp black slacks. His glasses were of a thickness that suggested he still thought it was the eighties. There were times when my friend and fellow desk clerk Otis would say that

Adam resembled a slightly heavier Stephen King, and I agreed with that sentiment completely.

"What's the scoop, Jessie?" Adam asked as he pushed his way through the glass door of the main entrance. His sense of calm made me think that he had been through the finding of a dead guest or two over the course of his time in the industry.

"I called the police and let 'em know," I reported as Adam entered the break room area.

"Okay, well, have some coffee or do whatever you need to calm down a bit, man. You know her or something?" Adam asked.

"Not at all," I answered.

"Then it's not your problem outside of your obligations here," Adam said in an attempt to comfort me with his cold logic.

The police came, and I comfortably went through the motions of explaining how I had come to find Ms. Edwards. Seeing as how business was as dead as the girl in 113, we conducted our conversation in the lobby in front of Abdul, the desk clerk that had relieved Samantha and was covering the second shift. Adam and I sat in the two chairs closest to the coffee bar while the two policemen sat with their backs to the elevator. The words came easily as I walked them through the process of getting to the point that would haunt me long after clocking out. I think I am at ease when speaking to the police because by the time they've made it to the property, they're wanted company. Happenings at the Blue Moon have brought the police around dozens of times in my years here, and my mind is typically at ease when I see them making rounds in the parking lot.

My foundation of apathy had been shaken as I felt something. Adam told me to clock out, go get my mind off of the day's events, and that he would take care of the bank deposit. Without any other obligations, I retrieved my wallet from my apartment and went out to pick up a twelve pack of beer, all of which would be consumed in an attempt to blur the memory of that day. To no avail; she haunts me still.

Once I had locked myself away in the fourth story apartment unit, I unplugged the room phone, turned off my cell, drank myself back to apathy, and hoped that my first time finding a body would be my last.

2

I awoke at six o'clock the following morning for a desk shift that was scheduled to start at seven. Brewing a pot of coffee before showering, I shaved my face and toasted an everything bagel that I lightly buttered; it was the first thing that I had eaten in two days, and I devoured it very quickly in spite of my stomach's alcohol induced uneasiness. Thankful that the blur of the alcohol had blanketed my dreams with darkness, her face burdened my thoughts upon awakening. Escaping the view from that inch and a half opening would be attempted through many bottles, but would only be replaced by something with a value greater than a single life.

When I got down to the lobby, my maintenance guy Wolfgang and my night auditor Cheryl were talking behind the front desk. I had come down through the stairwell and was walking toward the main entrance area when I heard Cheryl's blaring voice in the volume which she was accustomed to speaking. Damn that woman was loud.

Wolfgang had interrupted his own conversation with Cheryl to greet me, "Gut morgen Mr. President. How are you?" Wolfgang asked before making his daily offer, "I've got caffe in the back for you."

"Thanks, man, I'm gonna need more than I had upstairs if I want to get the day started," I said before responding to his question, "I'm doin alright. How was your day off?" I didn't give him the chance to answer before I went to the back area and clocked in.

"It was pretty good, man," Wolfgang said as I swiped my time card, "my soccer team won five ta three and mah lady was there to watch. After that, we go back to her house and drink. Good off day, sir."

"That's awesome, man! Your team won! You fight anyone?" I asked. Wolfgang was accustomed to losing his temper while in the act of sport and has told a few stories. Any minor slight was interpreted as blatant disrespect, and was typically met with a direct challenge.

Born in the former Czech Republic, Wolfgang grew up in Germany. He was the prime example of perfect middle-aged health, as he found himself approaching fifty and still played in a local soccer league that primarily consisted of men in their thirties. Having grown up in Europe, he spoke at least five languages and even claimed on a few occasions to interpret tapped phone calls in Russian for the FBI. Wolfgang had only lived in the United States for about ten years to this point, but he had adapted to the culture quite well, considering his lifestyle. A man that speaks with an accent has an automatic advantage over his fellow man when it comes to the pursuit of sex, and his Eastern European accent layered over the fact that English was far from his second or third languages made women melt in his hands. I've actually watched it happen in front of me. While Wolfgang was married with an adult son in his twenties, he had a sugar momma on the side. Based on previous encounters of revealed mystery cash, Adam, Otis, and I were all pretty sure that he was a male prostitute that marketed himself to middle-aged women. More power to him. He rarely involved the hotel in his side operation. I've only ever met one of his regulars, an upper middle class woman who was married and had a teenage daughter. They had been involved with each other on the basis that he provides company and affection and she pay him pretty much whatever and whenever he asked. He literally demanded fourteen hundred dollars one time, and before the work day was up, Wolfgang produced the fourteen crisp one hundred dollar bills for my envy. Wolfgang carried a deeply held misogynistic double standard as he hated women who strayed from committed relationships while paying no respect to his own. This gender divide justified every action he carried out and excused him from responsibility.

"Nah," Wolfgang laughed, "no one

really pissed me off. Too busy kicking ass on the field," he said as he punched at the air. He then stopped and changed his expression to something more serious as he asked if I were alright.

"Yeah, I'm good," I sighed as I filled a mug with coffee from the batch Wolfgang had brewed. "Adam tell you about yesterday, or something?"

"No. Cheryl. She said Samantha told her about you finding dead girl in room."

I shrugged as I nodded my head, "Yeah, it was pretty shitty. I called the police and dealt with that, but as soon as the police business was done, Adam let me take off the rest of the shift."

"Jesus Christ," Wolfgang started, "why do you think people do that to themselves? You know, I never do drugs in life! I only drink, and I used to smoke regular cigarettes. But why do people," Wolfgang made a motion that mimicked injection, "why would want to do that?"

I answered him as honestly as I could in saying, "People always tend to hurt themselves in one way or another. All I know is that when I got the door cracked and saw her lying there..." I shook my head as I trailed off.

"Shit. How you doing, today?" Wolfgang asked.

I lifted my cup and said, "I'm good, man. Got my coffee, should be a slow Monday, and I slept pretty well. I feel good, overall," I lied.

"That's good, man. If you need drink, I can bring you shots?" Wolfgang nodded as he made the offer. "I go next door and call you to run over and take shot real quick!"

"Thanks, Wolf, but not this early. I'll just have some coffee for now. Maybe we can step next door and get something after work?" I suggested.

"Perfect. I buy you shots. What you like? Jack Daniels?"

"Yeah, I could go for some Jack."

"You really gonna be drinkin' this early?" Cheryl howled from the open lobby area. She was the longest running employee at this particular Blue Moon Inn at nine solid years. She was consistently late and for that reason she was constantly at war with Otis. Otis was one of my best friends from my high school years, but I couldn't always tell what was fact and what he exaggerated as he explained things with the sensationalism of a journalist.

"After work," I clarified. "I can't keep it together behind the desk if I start drinking."

"You alright, Jessie?" Cheryl reached out to me as well.

"I'm good, I think. Thank you, Cheryl," I said through the morning haze.

"So what was it like?" She asked with the sudden twitch of her head.

"What was what like? Finding a dead girl in one of the rooms? It was fucking shitty! What do you think it's like?" I responded as though she were stupid.

There was an awkward silence before Cheryl said, "Well, I've gotta get to my other job," and left the front lobby area. She continued to speak as she emerged back into the lobby from the break room entrance, but I filtered out what I could only assume was noise. If a nod and an 'uh-huh' was good enough, I would be in the clear. "I mean, I just feel like I'm vulnerable here, ya know? Like I'm gonna get raped or something," she said as she made her exit.

A middle-aged man with a local ID wanted to pay cash for one of our least expensive rooms, which at that point was a standard double; comes with two double beds and runs for forty-nine, ninety-nine, plus tax. His ID identified him as John Williams, and his ring finger identified him as married. Having arrived at about nine thirty in the morning, I was lucky enough to have plenty of unsold rooms from Sunday clean and ready to rent. Everything was going well until I quoted him the total.

"How much?"

Repeating myself I politely recited, "After tax, it comes to fifty-eight, thirty-six."

The man hesitated in frustration before reaching into his pocket and pulling out five more dollars. "Sixty," he growled as he tossed the bill to the counter. "How high is the tax?"

Feeling that this situation could spiral out of control, I spoke cautiously, "Tax on hotel rooms in the city of Columbus is sixteen point seventy-five percent. It is painful."

"It's total bullshit!" the man cried in his outrage, his eyes creating a tension that expressed I was imposing such a tax to harm him. "It's bullshit! Obama and his whole Muslim administration would tax the air you breathe if he could!"

"I don't come to work to talk politics, sir," I said bluntly as the printer spit out his registration form.

"Well, I'm talkin' to ya! What'cha think about that?"

"I think that all of the taxes are set at the state level. Your receipt will show 'State' tax, 'County' tax, and a 'City' tax," I explained. "There is no federal collection on our revenue that you're paying for."

He signed the registration card and asked, "You got a problem with what I'm sayin'?"

"Mr. Williams," I sighed at the thought of moving forward in this empty headed rhetoric, "if you really want my honesty, I don't care what you think. At all."

"You should care; they're takin' away your rights! You smart enough to know that, right?"

"People that speak the loudest have made nothing but noise. You wanna know what I think, sir? Apathy defines the way I feel towards the whole process. I honestly don't care." I lied as I folded the reg card in half and slipped it into the black box that I would file numerically later in the day. I then programmed two keys for room 238, put them into a keycard envelope, labeled them with the assigned room number, and handed them to Mr. Williams. "Take the elevator to the second floor, make a left. Room's at the end of the hallway." I was moderately political and detested the party structure, but I get a far left or right weirdo in here from time to time. The best thing to do with those who try to corner the customer service guy with hard line partisan rhetoric is shoo them away as quickly as possible. I could indulge with this guy and say that if I controlled the land I would tax the air, but what good would it do when I'm stuck at the desk?

I recently had another guy down here asking me to print off lyrics to a song that he claimed to have written. The chord structure and lyrical setup suspiciously reminded me of *My Bonnie Lies over the Ocean* while the actual lyrics were about Mitt Romney and his off shore tax havens. It made me laugh, but only because I actually felt sorry for the old hippie. Upon handing him the printed copies of his song and with no other knowledge about me, he asked if this job was all I wanted to do with my life.

This job makes me hate people. Otis helped me to get a job at the Blue Moon, and to be honest, the perks make it not so bad. I get forty hours a week, health, visual, and dental insurance, a 401K, and enough free time to literally do what I want on the clock. I wish I could tell you that the political nuts are the worst of it, but prostitution and drug addicts looking for a place to get high are part of the day-to-day operation.

My favorite part of any work day were the periods of time in which I found myself completely alone. The opportunities were pretty endless. I'd typically get online at the start of the shift and read the news. Used to check the social networking sites, but I've since quit Facebook. I've read entire novels and have even completed a good portion of my college homework on the clock. Otis tends to use his free time to watch movies, but those extracurricular activities only account for surface value. Otis and I share a locker that is kept in the employee restroom. We keep a little bit of pot, a small one hitter the size of a cigarette, and a lighter stashed away in there for those really slow days. Sometimes I'll use a vacant room to smoke, other times I'll just sit in the stairwell, but the easiest places are in the laundry room or the room that hosts our fire alarm panel system as well as our wifi equipment that is found through a door inside of the storage closet in the laundry room.

Otis once told me about this incident where he got caught smoking on the job by the boss. He was in the stairwell, unaware that Adam had arrived. As Otis put the pipe to his lips, Adam entered the stairwell and silent eye contact was established between the two. Figuring he had already been caught and lost his job, Otis lights the pipe and takes a hit while Adam watched.

Shaking his head at such blatant stupidity, Adam scoffed, "Get back to work, you lazy piece of shit."

Otis then returned to the back office to screw around on the internet; defeated.

That should suffice in expressing how little our boss actually cared. He was negligent at best.

Adam arrived at ten o'clock, and he was only there that early because of the phone conference call meetings that were routinely scheduled for Mondays at eleven.

"What's going on, Jessie?" Adam

asked, "Today going any better for you?"

"Yeah man, thus far the body count for today is at zero."

"Let's keep it that way, fucker," he said as seriously as he could. "And not to get on your ass after a day like yesterday, but you've got to get their ID number on the registration card every time, every time, every time!"

"My bad, boss."

"It's cool. Anything going on here today?"

I shook my head and Adam went to the back area and into his office. I waited until he had his computer on before I spoke again, "I did have a guest freak out over the tax rate."

"Sweet," Adam smiled.

"No, that's not sweet! He started ranting about politics, but he seemed more like a troll trying to bait me with stupidity. It was just too stupid to be taken seriously. I finally got to the point where I issued him his keys and pretty much bailed on the conversation. Had to explain that I didn't care about the high tax rate."

Adam looked away from the computer and asked, "You do know why taxes on hotel rooms are high, don't you?"

"Yeah," I tried to play it off.

"You have no idea, do you?" He saw right through me.

"No idea," I echoed.

"Think about it," Adam explained, "what is it about hotel rooms that's different from restaurants, material possessions, or even cigarettes?" Adam paused as though I were supposed to suddenly get it. He sighed before continuing, "The only reason people in town get hotel rooms is because of an emergency, or more often, to fuck someone they shouldn't; they're either cheating, dealing in prostitution, or are involved with drugs. The majority of our target client base isn't local, and the city knows that. Why shouldn't we set high taxes on someone from Cleveland or Lexington? All cities have a high hotel tax rate. It's just another way to say, 'bring your money here!'"

"That makes total sense."

"No shit, Jessie. You got the bank deposit ready to go?"

"Haven't even popped the safe," I admitted.

"Lazy ass slacker. It'll have to wait until after the conference call," Adam said.

As Adam took his conference call, I checked in one of our regulars. She was a prostitute. After working here for as long as I have, it becomes apparent as to who does what. For a quick reference guide, I'll supply the side notes of 'How to Spot a Hooker: 101.' The first rule of thumb: a local ID plus paying in cash equates to some form of deviance. This alone doesn't seal the deal as they may just be cheating on their spouse or in need of privacy for whatever reason. Usually, not showing up with their client or secret lover, nine times out of ten they're texting during the check in process. The other person will arrive later and go straight to the room. Sometimes the man will check in and sometimes the woman but never together. The greatest detail to remove the blur from the lines of innocent cheating to full on prostitution would be if the guest becomes a regular and if the partner isn't consistently the same person. I've seen it often enough to develop the thickest of skin. I honestly don't care as long as you're discrete. The only time it really becomes a problem is when they start bringing in a lot of traffic. A high number of clients coming and going looks bad. None of the staff really cares whether or not you're a prostitute; you pay for the room, so do what you do. But as it is with any illegal activity, be discrete! I hate it when they start running marathons out of our rooms and act as though we're too stupid to know what they're up to. Not only does this nasty and illegal sex suggest we'll have to throw out all of the linen, but it also indicates a possible outlet for drug distribution as well, as we'll typically find crack pipes and used needles in the housekeeping aftermath.

On a handful of occasions I've had men actually complain that their wallet had been stolen by a prostitute. I literally looked one man in the eye and told him that if he didn't want to call the police, what was there for me to care about?

Sylvia Bobo was a prostitute and a regular at the Blue Moon Inn. She was middle-aged, a redhead, skinny, and freckled. Without the assistance of a pimp, I always worried for her safety. Then again, she had been at it at our location twice a week for the past two and a half years, and she seemed to manage just fine. She showed up twenty minutes into Adam's conference call that morning. The idea of her showing up just before noon led me to believe that she's on the job while her kids were at school.

Without the faintest glimpse of happiness she asked, "Boss gonna be in today?"

Knowing that Adam was preoccupied in the office, I lied and said, "Don't think so," as I made a key for a vacant room on the second floor. She then handed me half of what the room would usually cost. I pocketed it, and that was that. She had developed this under the table deal with Otis, and after putting up with his constant bragging, I wanted in. All we had to do was mark the room as 'dirty' and either Adam didn't care enough to do a thorough job with the reports, or he just didn't care at all. It was a profitable little operation of which I regularly enjoyed the fruits.

Adam ended up leaving for the bank fifteen minutes before Otis was to start his shift.

When Otis arrived, he started complaining almost immediately, "Don't wanna be here today," he said as he puffed on his inhaler and walked along the counter. His asthma was a real issue for him, and the health insurance this place provided was the only reason that he still worked there. His long brown hair and glasses were the only traits that we had in common, and yet it was more than enough to drive the majority of our guests to confuse us for each other. He was taller than me by a few inches, had broader shoulders, and just to be a jerk, his nose was bulbous when compared to mine. If we weren't mistaken for each other, we were mistaken for brothers. We weren't even born in the same country as I'm an Ohioan, and Otis was born in a small town near Dublin, Ireland. He moved to the States with his mother before starting grade school, and as a result, he spoke with the accent of any other suburban kid in the Midwest. His Irish accent only surfaced when he had been drinking heavily, which was rare for me to hear as our work schedules cut into the time that we used to hang out.

"You never wanna be here," I responded as he walked past the counter.

"Especially now! Fall weather is so perfect. Look how nice it is out there. That's what I have to look at for the next eight hours," he said as he clocked in.

"Always bitching," I pointed out as the elevator opened.

There was five seconds of hesitation and the elevator door started to close when it was stopped, and Penelope Rice of 329 stepped out and into the lobby. She was three hours late on paying to stay over, but Adam rarely put forth effort to get rid of someone holding up until the second shift had started. She looked like a greasy mess as she shambled to the counter. Everything about her looked dirty except for the fresh coat of bright orange nail polish that caused the tips of her fingers to glow.

"Hey there," I said.

She reached her hand into her low cut sweater and removed cash from her bra as she asked, "Can I pay for another night?"

"Sure," I said to the poor junkie. She looked wired and fatigued at the same time. Her makeup reminded me of the girl I had found the day before as her eyes were craters to a soulless vessel. "It'll be the same as last night, fifty-two, fifty-two."

"Thanks, sweetie," Penelope said as she set the cash down on the counter, "and hey, tell Otis I said 'hi' okay?"

"You got it."

It wasn't until after Penelope had received new room keys and was back on the elevator that Otis came to the front desk area. "Thanks, man. I did not want to deal with her just yet."

"No problem. But I feel you on that; I don't want to deal with her either. By the way, she says-"

"Shut the fuck up!" Otis cut me off.

"What do you think is going on in there?" I asked.

"Terrible things, Jessie. Stop thinking. Right now!" Otis laughed at the horrible truth.

I told Otis about finding the dead girl in 113.

"I checked her in, man. Damn. You never think these things are gonna happen," Otis said.

"Tell me about it. You're pretty much the last person to know outside of the housekeepers. Pretty much trickled down from shift to shift, so I figured I'd tell you about it myself."

Otis shrugged, "I can appreciate it."

"Worst part is Wolfgang heard it from Cheryl," I started.

"Christ," Otis said. "What did the telephone game turn it into by the time she started telling people?"

"I'm not really sure. Don't think she distorted what little information there is, but as she was rambling this morning she expressed that she now fears for her safety. Said something about being raped."

"Ain't nobody gonna rape her unless they pull a rape/suicide."

"You are the worst person I know," I laughed.

At this point, a dirty yellow Ford F150 pickup truck pulled into our parking lot. It glided with a slow caution before parking as far away from the main entrance as possible. The driver was a man who appeared to be in his late forties, possibly fifties. His female passenger appeared to be at least ten years younger, but as she approached the lobby, her face expressed an aging that carried the weight of heavy drug use.

As soon as the woman stepped out of the truck, Otis asked, "You know what they're here for?"

"How much do you think he's paying her?" I returned his question with one of my own.

"Who gives a shit? I fucking hate these trashy people, man. You check 'em in!" Otis said as he ducked back into the office. "I can't believe he's actually waiting in the truck! It's so obvious, it's not even funny."

When she walked in alone, her eyes searched in a desperate paranoia before she opened her mouth to speak, "How much is a room for the night?"

My response was mechanical as I recited, "After tax, our least expensive is fifty-eight, thirty-six."

"Okay," she started, "I've been a guest here before, and I was wondering if I'd be needin' to show ID to get a room?"

"Yes," I explained, "whoever is going to sign for the room has to show me a photo ID."

"Thanks," she said as she started walking towards the back door next to the stairwell. She then slipped out, went left, and was gone.

"What in the hell?" Otis trailed off as he realized what had just happened.

"I dunno, man. I think she took his money and ran!"

Otis smiled as it sank in, "Fucking sweet!"

"Yeah," I agreed.

The guy in the truck sat there for another ten solid minutes. My shift had ended, and Otis had officially taken over, but I had nowhere better to be. When the guy did finally get out of his truck, he walked with a conviction that seemed to overcome his previous hesitation.

"Hey there," Otis said as the man entered.

He cut right to the chase, "Did a woman just check in?"

Still behind the counter, I answered him, "A woman wanted to check in. I told her that she would need a photo ID for the room, and she left. Went out through the back door."

There was a moment of tense and awkward silence. Then suddenly from his mouth came the most disappointed and pathetic sounding, "Son of a bitch," I've ever heard.

As soon as the door had shut behind him, Otis and I broke out into rampant laughter.

"Hey, man, Wolfgang wants to buy me a couple of drinks next door, so I'm gonna go and try to forget about yesterday. I'll be back through in a while," I said to Otis as I clocked out.

When I arrived at the Mexican restaurant next door to the hotel, Wolfgang and Adam were already in the middle of a pitcher of margaritas. "Mr. President!" Wolfgang announced happily as I approached the bar. Aside from the Mexican eatery, there was also another bar next to the Blue Moon, but Wolfgang was friends with most of the workers at the restaurant as a few of them played in the same soccer league.

"Have a seat, you poor bastard," Adam said as he motioned for the attention of the bartender.

"Thanks, man," I said as I sat to Adam's left.

"Yeah, we need a glass for him and another pitcher of margarita," Adam said to the bartender. "We're gonna be here a while," Adam said as he turned his attention to Wolfgang and me.

"Why are you sticking around so late?" I asked in genuine confusion.

Adam shook his head as he answered

with a question, "You really think I want to go home to a wife that fuckin' hates me? These moments are the highlight of my day."

Wolfgang nodded to show he could relate.

When I went back to the hotel, I was drunk enough to just want to make my way to my apartment unit. Looking straight forward, I was gunning it for the elevator when Otis emerged from the back office.

"Hey, Otis. How's it going?" I said as I stopped at the counter. His body language indicated that he wanted to talk.

"Jessie, you drunk?" Otis asked before lifting his inhaler to his mouth and taking a puff.

"Yes, sir," I gave a nod and smirked.

"Well, do you remember Jeremy Cross? Douche bag that ran with the party crowd after high school."

"That guy always hated me, and I never really knew why," I slurred. "I mean, I heard different things from different people, but every single person I ever talked to about it confirmed that he just flat out loathed my existence. I mean, when I slept with 'what's er name' I was under the impression that she was single!"

Otis looked me in the eye and said in all seriousness, "Well, he stopped in while you were out with Wolfgang. Said Penelope and the others are cooking meth up in 329."

"Fuck," I muttered. "You sure? I mean, when the source is Jeremy Cross..." I paused and rolled my eyes, "see why I'm skeptical?" Pretty sure that I was slurring my words, I repeated myself just to be on the safe side, "See why I'm skeptical?"

Otis nodded, "Yeah, I get that much, but it's reason enough to get those freaks out of here!"

"You're serious? They're cooking meth up in 329?" I asked hazily as I was not grasping the seriousness or showing the proper sense of urgency that's associated with hearing that kind of information.

"Yes Jessie," Otis slowly reiterated, "they're cooking crystal meth in 329."

Smiling wide I said, "That's nice," and I'm not kidding. That was actually the last thing I said to Otis before I got on the elevator, took it to the third floor, and took the stairs from there to my apartment where I promptly passed out. My excuse at that point was that we had nothing to go on but the word of another guy who ran with the hard drug crowd. Apathy can be a wonderful thing, especially when it consumes me.

Fully clothed, I awoke with my head pounding at ten thirty-five that night. I couldn't believe that I had consumed as much alcohol as I did, but hard liquor will have her way with me. That, and Wolfgang is a pusher. He has insisted that he buy and I drink more on every occasion that I have been out drinking with him. As my eyes adjusted to the darkness, I realized that Otis would be at the end of his shift. I rolled to my left and suffered a head rush that caused a sharp pain. This was one nasty hangover. Collecting myself, I breathed deeply and tightened my stomach. Once I realized that I wasn't yet going to vomit, I picked up the receiver and hit '0' to call the front desk.

He picked up after one ring; his delivery was a tired and typical monotone. "Guest services, this is Otis, how may I help you?"

"Hey, man, it's me," I groaned, "I just woke up and had to call because I wanted to be sure that it wasn't just me being drunk but,"

"Yeah," Otis intervened, "We did have a conversation about Jeremy Cross admitting that Penelope and the others are up there making drugs."

"So, they're cooking meth in there, huh?"

"To the best of my knowledge. I had a guest staying near them complain about the smell in the hall. I went up there and it sure as shit doesn't smell right. Hint of sulfur, among other things."

"Shit. I guess I'll give the police a call now. Sorry about earlier, man. I was a bit too drunk to grasp the reality of what you were saying," I said.

"Excuses. Excuses, you lazy bastard!" Otis scolded.

"Something like that," I responded before hanging up.

Not knowing when 329 would be wrapping up their operation, I figured that I would have to call and deal with the authorities immediately. I couldn't risk them checking out the next day, and I was actually angry that these scumbags would use this place to test the depths to which they could sink. With a Sig Sauer pistol that I had stashed in my bread drawer, it would be so easy to make a key to their room, barge right in, and make the world a better place. But that approach would be so easily traced as I had just purchased the gun for self defense since receiving the promotion less than a year earlier, and every key that gets made is documented in an electronically based systematic report. Unfortunately, this fantasy is just that- something that I will never get to carry out. I actually got out of bed and started to brew a pot of coffee with the intent to sober up a bit more before having to talk to someone legitimately. I would again call Adam before contacting the police.

I feel terrible throwing him under the bus in saying that he was a lousy boss when these scenarios I'm sharing show quite the opposite. He answered his phone at eleven o'clock in the evening, "It's late. This better be good."

"It's real good," I replied.

"Details, Jessie. Spit it out before I hang up on you."

"It's been told to Otis that the guests in 329 are cooking up meth in the room."

There were two seconds of silence before Adam simultaneously exhaled and said, "Shit."

"Shit, indeed."

"You think the source has credibility?" Adam asked.

"I wasn't sure, but Otis said he has had another guest complain of the smell at the end of the hallway," I reported. "Sorry to bother you with this, but I just wanted to run it by you before I called the police."

Adam sighed, "Don't worry about it, man. I'll take care of it."

"You're gonna call the police for me and come take care of it?" I was surprised.

"Yeah, man. After telling me that sort of thing, there's no way I couldn't opt to personally address the situation."

"Thanks," I said.

"No problem. See you in the morning, fucker," Adam said before hanging up on me.

I was lucky to have gotten back to sleep around three in the morning as I had a desk shift scheduled to start at seven.

When I clocked in at six fifty-seven, Adam was already in the back office. To see him this early was a very rare occasion. Cheryl was borderline silent as a result, an even rarer occurrence. I drew a mug of coffee from the thermos in the break room that Wolfgang had recently brewed.

"Coffee good this morning, Mr. President?" Wolfgang asked as I took a drink.

"Yeah, man, it's just what I needed. Hey, Adam, what are you doing here this early?"

Adam turned away from the computer and faced me, "We're expecting a visit from the local branch of the DEA this morning. I wanted to be here when they raid 329. You know, in case we end up with another body on our hands or something."

"Oh wow, man, so they're still in there?" I asked.

"You really think they're gonna bail at midnight when check out isn't until noon?"

"Good point," I said as I turned my attention to a guest in the lobby.

It was five minutes after nine when two black vans with the words "Drug Enforcement Agency" on the sides in white pulled into our parking lot. The first one parked next to the glass door at the far end of the building that was closest to 329 and the stairwell that went straight to their hallway. The other came through the underpass and pulled into the first spot, facing the Mexican restaurant. It was another twenty to thirty seconds before five men emerged from the van facing the restaurant. They wore solid black riot gear that was padded with the outline of bullet proof vests beneath the surface of their clothing. All but one were wearing gas masks. The man without a gas mask was the only one not carrying an automatic weapon. He had a pistol at his side and was wearing aviator sunglasses. With the window of room 329 facing the front end of the building, the agents from the closest van moved in quickly while the other van remained idle.

Once in the lobby, the man with the aviators came up to the counter to speak with Adam while the others waited next to the elevator. While Adam was standing next to me, I could feel the judgmental glare coming through the reflecting lenses.

"They still up there?" the agent asked Adam while still looking through me.

"To the best of my knowledge," my boss answered with a confidence that I just couldn't grasp in that moment. "I went up there fifteen minutes ago and heard some kind of activity that wasn't noise from the television."

"Alright," said the man in aviators before turning his attention to his crew, "let's do this. Schwab and White, you guys take the stairwell in case they already know about us and are trying to gun it outta here. Wilkus, Johnson, and I will take the elevator and meet you on the third floor to go from there, providing there's no complications on the stairs or elevator." He then turned his attention back to us in asking, "Where's the stairwell?"

"Last door on the left," I gestured down the hall.

"Make them a key to the room," Adam ordered.

I nodded and programmed one of our plastic card keys for room 329. I then offered it to the guy with the aviators who aggressively snatched it from my hand.

Without any verbal response, two of the men began to head towards the stairs. Wilkus or Johnson pressed the button for the elevator which opened immediately.

Once the elevator door had closed behind the DEA agents, the side doors to the second van opened and seven or eight men in gas masks poured out of it. With their weapons already drawn, they went into the glass door that didn't require a key to enter during the daylight hours.

"Remember, Jessie," Adam sighed, "if anyone representing the media contacts you about this or the dead girl you found, you tell 'em that you can't comment on anything, and give them the corporate media hotline number."

"I know the drill," I responded.

What felt like an eternity was over in twenty minutes. I saw the entire crew of DEA agents leave through the glass door at the end of the building. With them were the two men that were staying in the room with Penelope. The man in aviators made his way back to the lobby and asked Adam if there was a better place where they could talk. Adam went with him to the third floor suite where they discussed details that later trickled down to me.

The end result was that they were in fact cooking crystal meth in the room and had been for a few days after properly setting up. Zero casualties, but Penelope was not in the room or found during the raid. According to the guys, they hadn't seen Penelope since the previous evening, but the authorities weren't buying it and were looking to pressure them on her whereabouts.

Housekeepers were individually instructed by Adam to stay out of there as we had to put the room out of order. It would be the second room this week that would require an outside company to come in for some sort of specialty cleaning, 113 for dead body procedure, and now 329 due to the leftover chemical cocktails of a meth operation. We were instructed to stay out of the room as the chemical leftovers could be hazardous to the point of causing an explosion.

I informed Otis of the day's events when he arrived for his shift. Adam had since gone home, and because it was doubtful that he'd return that day, Otis had intrigued my curiosity about the state of the room. With it being a borderline dead Tuesday afternoon, Otis and I decided to check it out.

Abandoning the front desk, we had left a sign that informed any potential walk-in that we were helping another guest and would return in a timely manner.

We came to find a sign the size of a piece of notebook paper had been placed on the door to room 329. It was a solid red sticker with black lettering that read, "U.S. Department of Justice. Drug Enforcement Administration. WARNING-A clandestine laboratory for the manufacture of illegal drugs and/or hazardous chemicals was seized at this location on (space for date left blank). Known hazardous chemicals have been disposed of pursuant to law. However, there still may be hazardous substances or waste products on this property, either in buildings or in the ground itself. Please exercise caution while on these premises. U.S. Department of Justice. Drug Enforcement Administration. Phone: (space for number left blank). -WARNING. DEA Form-483 (Mar. 1988)."

"Otis, check this out!" I said as I gestured toward the sign.

An insanely large smile broke out across Otis' face as he slurred the word, "Cool."

"Holy shit, this is gonna be bad for business," I followed up.

"Who cares? Business is already slow

enough. We're a pit, and anyone who gets a room on this end of the smoking floor knows it and is more than likely here for our pit-like qualities. You really think one of our regulars like Von Hertz is going to give a fuck?"

"Probably not someone like Von Hertz," I started, "but we get randoms up here all the time. Nothing we can really do about it, though. So I'm not going to worry about it."

"Well?" Otis inquired vaguely through an inflection in his tone.

"Well, what?" I asked, genuinely confused.

Otis looked at me as though I were truly that stupid and asked, "Did we come up here to check out this super cool poster the DEA left, or are we gonna check out the wreckage?"

"Wreckage it is," I said as I used the plastic card key to open the lock. Turning the handle and opening the door, I couldn't believe that three people had dwelled there for close to a week in that horror show.

The raid had been conducted at such a rate that only the actual cooking equipment was confiscated while bits of crystal meth were left scattered among the garbage and debris that was made up of fast food containers and snack wrappers. Little cloudy white pebble looking pieces were dotted along the countertop next to the television. The smell of the room was disgusting, not only due to the chemical mess they had made, but for two other reasons; it seemed as though they had stopped showering during their stay and some of the fast food wrappers must have contained leftovers that had been in a state of decomposition or whatever fast food does. Even the beds were littered with bits of trash and cigarette butts.

"This is just fucking terrible!" Otis laughed as he scanned the room for the most disgusting offenses.

"Yeah, it is," I said as I looked over crystal meth for the first time. I suddenly felt nauseated and in awe of the weight that this sort of thing carried.

"You alright, Jessie?" Otis asked. He must have interpreted my glare at the drugs as carrying some kind of desire, "You're not actually going to do anything with that shit, are you?"

"No, man. I haven't done anything hard in a number of years, and I've never done anything like meth. It's just weird to see up close," I explained. I carry a certain amount of disgust in the idea of trying it as I had always considered meth to be a dirty and greasy drug.

"Good. Dude, check out the bathroom!" Otis laughed again. He was truly entertained.

I took one look in the bathroom and lightened up at the sight of a tub that they had turned into a trash can and ashtray. I laughed and said, "I thought it smelled like they gave up showering! What is wrong with people?"

Otis used his inhaler and didn't reply to the question as he said, "Let's get the fuck outta here! I gotta get back to the desk." Without waiting for a reply, Otis turned and promptly left the ruins of this once successful operation. "Can't believe we work at this shit-hole."

Alone in what had been a meth lab a few short hours earlier, I breathed deeply and exhaled as I wished that this was the bottom. Limitless are the depths we sink.

3

Quitting my job felt like an impulsive desire that I just could not fulfill. The neighborhood was considered a good part of town, but five minutes south was a terribly bad area. I would not want the same job in most places, but at this point I was too far in to quit on the spot. We could talk forever about the poor state of the economy and how this job didn't pay very well, but I was living on the property and figured the moment I resign is the moment I'm kicked out of my apartment. Days would sometimes go by and I wouldn't leave the property! I was far too invested, I know that much now.

Otis called my apartment phone at nine thirty that night from the front desk, "Dude, Von Hertz just checked into 326. Put down fifty dollars for movies."

"That's terrible, man. Gross. You've just ruined my dinner," I said into the receiver.

"Whatever, man, you wanted to know."

"No, I didn't!" I shouted. "Although it has been forever since we saw him last. Honestly, I thought he was either dead or in jail."

"Looks like jail. Got a mug shot online from a few months back- possession," Otis replied.

Murdock Von Hertz was a regular who had been staying at our property long before I started working there. Local ID. Paid in cash. Never brought a sexy time partner or extra traffic of any kind. He kept quiet and to himself as most of the 'paranoid for a reason' types usually do. He'd get a smoking room with a king size bed, and he never got one of the ground floor smoking kings. Always on the third floor. As he checks in, he'll set down an extra twenty to seventy dollars for our shitty brand of motel porn offered in the pay per view options. In the month of November, 2009, he spent twelve hundred dollars at our establishment on rooms and pornography alone. There were stretches where he'd be checked in for days at a time. He'd leave during the day and return that night with more unquestioned cash. Von Hertz always relocated the armchair into a position that would put the TV into a better view. Never slept in the bed, never showered in our facilities, and never left anything that could have been considered reason enough to ban him from staying. As with most, Von Hertz's creepy attributes only existed because we literally knew nothing about him other than that a mug shot website confirmed he had been issued a charge for possession of a controlled substance in 2005, as well as the recent charge Otis had described.

Otis had tried once to set up an under the table operation with Von Hertz, but it came with the complication that if he wasn't actually registered, how would he be able to order pornography? This hindered Otis from establishing more shady endeavors to undercut the place and pocketing cash on the spot. I never understood why he paid to rent the movies when the wifi was free.

The next morning a housekeeper requested maintenance in room 326. Not speaking English well, Estela simply asked, "Wolf come to 326?"

"Yes," I answered into the receiver.

When I asked Wolfgang if he would check it out, he went up to the room and quickly returned.

"Shit, Jessie. What de fuck? Iz eh handicapped?" Wolfgang asked, but he asked this sort of thing regularly, and I didn't really consider that anything was out of the ordinary.

"Who's handicapped?" I asked.

Wolfgang looked to the floor and sneered, "326." He then made a gesture to imply masturbation as he said, "Bitch!"

"Von Hertz?"

"Yeah, man, come upstairs, and look at the way he left it," Wolfgang waved to encourage leaving the desk.

"Alright," I said as I put the sign on the counter.

We took the stairs to the third floor and then to Von Hertz's room to find that the microwave, mini fridge, alarm clock, phone, and television were all unplugged from their corporate appointed outlets. Wolfgang and I also found the low-end motel art had been removed from their spots on the wall and placed on the floor underneath the air conditioning unit. The mirror above the dresser had been taken down in a similar fashion. Besides the few items out of place, the room was clean. The bed was made and pulled as tightly as our housekeepers are trained, the shower stall was dry with the white towels neatly folded on the edge of the tub to reveal a packet of shampoo and soap, and the two trash cans were left completely untouched.

"What is wrong with this creature?" Wolfgang asked.

My eyes moved across the room as I really considered my options before answering, "He thinks we're watching him."

Adam finally arrived toward the end of my desk shift. Pouring himself a cup of black coffee, he seethed with the tension that he brought from home. Wolfgang tried to talk to him about their mutual hatred for LeBron James, but Adam was too preoccupied with a developing hatred of his wife. He took a seat in his office and sighed deeply. Adam then claimed that a corporate guest would be staying at our property and asked me to make a gratis reservation for Friday, my day off.

"No problem, man. What's goin on?" I asked as I keyed in the reservation.

"Robert Martinez is coming in. I'm not quite sure as to what kind of business he's conducting. Might want to go over our property, might want to get away from his wife with a couple of fat girls," Adam answered.

Robert Martinez was the area manager and was known to bring young girls, mainly prostitutes, to the hotels he visited while on business that required him to stay overnight. There were also times when he would take petty cash from the property safe and use it to pay the ladies. Higher up the ladder, Robert's immediate boss was a friend with whom he had conducted business over the previous twenty plus years. These little indulgences were overlooked on a level that high. Even disgruntled employees kept their mouths shut as Martinez appeared untouchable.

"Hey, Adam, Von Hertz stayed with us last night."

"What's new?" Adam sneered.

I told him about the activities of our paranoid guest.

There were a couple seconds of silence before Adam muttered, "You piece of shit." He then looked up and asked, "Why do you think Von Hertz is unplugging everything and removing the wall art? I mean, really? What could be that far up his ass?"

"He's looking for something that would imply surveillance, an audio or visual recording device. Thinks we're watching him while he jacks off."

"Why do the weirdoes flatter themselves?" Adam gave me a look. "I mean, you're a piece of shit, and your ego's bigger than your dick! I just don't get it."

"He's probably up to some kind of hard drug use and actually thinks the police might show up while he's in the middle of whatever..." I trailed off.

"Fuck," Adam said without emotion. "The housekeepers are gonna find him dead one day."

"Wouldn't be surprised."

Based on my sleep schedule, I crashed out as soon as Otis arrived for his shift. I had been feeling depressed since finding Ms. Edwards in 113. Witnessing bits of the DEA raid and the aftermath of the meth lab didn't help in easing my stress. As I drank a glass of water before going to sleep, I thought about what kept me at this shit job.

Conclusions surface. Things like after getting my BA in history and having no motivation to go further in order to pursue a teaching career as planned resulted in this job being all that I had left. My parents had moved near the coast in North Carolina, and we seldom spoke as I had been labeled the 'troubled' of their three children. I had also lost touch with Elyse, my lady friend through college, as she had also moved forward with her life. She had been accepted to pursue a PHD program at New York University, and we haven't spoken since she left. That was over two years ago. This job is all I have left to help identify myself. This wretched harbor of human waste has hardened my heart to the point that it could be used to bludgeon a man to death, and yet it was the only place where I could find comfort. That was the absolute worst feeling of all.

Otis called me about an hour into his shift. I had finally slipped away from consciousness when that damn thing rang and again robbed me of sleep.

"Hello," I said unhappily into the receiver.

There was an excitement in Otis' voice that disregarded my tone as he said, "Best housekeeper find, ever!"

"What?" I hazily inquired. I wanted him to hear that I wasn't thrilled about this call if it didn't require my immediate attention.

"Estela brought down a diary that was left in a room on the third floor last night. I flipped through it before filing it away, and it's just crazy."

"Details, man," I demanded impatiently.

"It's the diary of a stripper who also happens to be a junkie."

A smile finally broke the surface as I could only muster the response of, "You're fuckin' kiddin' me. Don't get my hopes up!"

"No way, man."

"How long is it?" I asked.

"It's only about ten pages, but she covers everything. Talks about getting and doing drugs, falling in love as soon as she fucks someone new, and hating herself!" There was such excitement in his voice that I wasn't quite sure whether or not he would be able to contain his junkie exposing joy.

"Otis, I need you to put it in the locker," I started. "I'm too tired to come down and check it out right now, but I work the desk shift in the morning. I totally want to read that, man! Please, Otis, put that in our shared locker so I can read it tomorrow."

"What if she comes back for it?" Otis asked.

"Then return the property to her. I'll have missed my chance. Not that big of a deal," I said.

"Oh, man. It is that big a deal. But sure, Jessie, I'll leave it in the locker for you."

"Thanks, man," I said.

"No problem. Take it easy." Otis' enthusiasm had deflated before hanging up the phone.

I kept the receiver pressed to my ear for ten seconds after the line had gone dead. Placing the receiver on the nightstand so that I wouldn't be bothered, I knew that Otis had worked there long enough to hold everything down.

Thursday started with my usual routine. I clocked in and got a mug of Wolfgang's coffee. I then went to the front desk and started preparing the housekeeping charts for the day. After distributing rooms and assigning the boards, I was surprised to find Cheryl actually leaving instead of hanging around. As soon as the door had closed behind her, I ran to the restroom and opened the locker that Otis and I had shared. Our mint tin which we used to store an emergency work stash was sitting on top of a journal-sized book. The cover was blank, and the texture felt like some sort of hardened fabric. In awe, I slowly lifted it out of the locker and took it to the office, sat down, turned off the heating unit, as Cheryl tended to abuse the damn thing, set the book to the desk, and opened the front cover. To my delight, there were Polaroid pictures of old stuffed animals, two in the front cover, and two in the back. Most of the stuffed animals looked to have been through some serious wear and tear over the years. These must've been a nostalgic reminder of some distant childhood. The content of the pages within would not reflect such happy memories.

As it turned out, Von Hertz had stayed with us for the second night in a row. Based on the time that he left and then returned, we had cleaned 326 and rented it to someone else, resulting in Von Hertz checking into a different room, 323. It was in there that he had earned himself a new single night record of seven porno movies ordered from our services. He was due to check out, and once it hit noon I automatically went through the process of doing so. Seeing seven different hits with the single night's stay, I couldn't resist the urge to print up a copy of his receipt to show Otis.

Another thing I couldn't resist was the urge to inspect the room. The housekeeper assigned to the third floor had not yet gotten to 323, and as it turned out, I found that Von Hertz had managed to unplug the television, phone, fridge, and every light that was plugged in. Having pulled the mini fridge out of its place embedded in the same structure that held the dresser, he moved it to the furthest corner of the room. The final thing he did, which was another step in the 'paranoid' direction, was that he unscrewed every light bulb in the room and bathroom and neatly set them in a row on top of the work desk like a collection on display.

"You think that's fucked up, you should read my diary!" Adam laughed as he closed the book and set it on the desk in the back office. He seemed tense that day and I figured he could use a laugh.

"Know what else is fucked up?" I asked as Otis was clocking in.

"Coming from you, I don't really want to know," Adam said.

"Fine, I'll just tell Otis, and if you happen to overhear, I don't really care," I announced.

"Huh, what's goin on?" Otis inquired.

"First, I showed Adam the diary."

Otis suddenly laughed and broke the ice of dreading the coming shift, "Awesome!"

"But moving forward, I've got something that might match the depths of the diary."

Adam intervened, "Jessie, you are such a douche bag."

"Speaking of douche bags, you guys wouldn't believe this guy that came in earlier." I announced.

"Why, what was he doing?" Otis asked cautiously.

"Looking for a job," I answered.

"Aren't we all?" Adam laughed in

terrifying honesty.

"For real," I nodded before moving forward, "but you've gotta hear me out. So he asks if we're hiring. I told him we weren't and routinely followed it up with the ol 'it doesn't hurt to fill out an application if you've got the time' spiel." A smile broke out across my face as I continued, "He hesitated before tripping all over his story, 'I-I've only been out of prison f-for four months, and I spent the p-past twenty-five years there. That won't automatic-tic-ally cut me out, will it?'"

"Oh, shit," Otis' imagination was starting to run with the possibilities.

"I wasn't sure, but I told him that it wouldn't automatically disqualify him from the hiring process. He gave me a nod and I gave him an app. He filled it out in the lobby and well," I paused as I grabbed the application from the back office, "you guys have got to check this out!"

Otis' eyes searched the piece of paper for the crime inquiry section. He then laughed uncontrollably for close to ten seconds before he read the words out loud, "'Nineteen eighty-five: five counts of rape. Sexual contact w/two cousins. Five to twenty-five years. 06/04/1987-07/28/2012' What the fuck is wrong with people?"

"He could've written 'sex offender.' Could've written 'convicted of rape,' but did he have to tell us that it was with his cousins?"

"His own family." Otis was shocked by the weight of it. He then changed the subject suddenly, "You showed boss the diary, so that means she hasn't been back for it?"

I shook my head, "Haven't heard from her. Give me a call if she shows up for it, and I'll bring it down."

"What are you going to do with it?" Otis asked.

"I'm gonna type it up so that we'll have a record of this thing!"

"Pages will be all stuck together. You're gonna spank it when she talks about heroin and hating herself. Admit it!" Otis pointed at me to accompany his accusing tone.

Truth is I did type up the majority of what was legible. Most of the diary was rambling garbage, but I did run across a few excerpts that I found to be interesting. I felt bad for this poor girl. Her name was Chelsie.

So he called me on Thursday while I was at work and told me he couldn't do it anymore, it was too stressful, goodbye. I was so upset I cried (at work) and it ruined my mood all night. So I didn't make any $. I've called him a few times since to get my shit back and he just threatening to beat me up if I come to his studio w/a cop, so he'd have to give it to me.
Now, about Eric and Karia...

On Halloween we all had a 3some. It was my first one, and I loved it. Since then, Eric and I have developed a 'thing' for each other (he/she just broke up yesterday) and over the last week she's been a lying, raging, psycho bitch. So now I'm sitting in a

Taco Bell parking lot waiting for the Mexicans to get here w/the dope.

Well I don't know what happened to that last entry. Guess I got too busy. Pretty high, must be careful. Junkie. Not me. Never. Hope not. Self control. Steve just left. Sold him dope a few days ago and don't feel so good about that. Protect the ones you care for. Must do better.

I realized/remembered that I used to be such a free spirit. I didn't dislike black people (or anyone for that matter; I was very accepting). I never cared about makeup or hair extensions or getting my nails done. I had a great self-image and I was always pleasant to be around. I miss THAT me- the real me. I can think of 3 major things why I'm not like that anymore.

1) Heroin. That was the first thing. It pretty much numbs everything and shuts down any lively personality. It started out @ Josh's house, but then it was basically a habit rather than an addiction. But now that I live with Karla & Eric, I started shooting it. It's only been 3 weeks now, but I'm sure it won't be long until it's n addiction, which is the reason I've been cutting down-so it doesn't. I refuse to be a junkie.

2) Being a stripper. Everyone who knew me before I decided to do this was shocked when they found out. I am too when I think about it. Like I said, I've never been interested in heels or hair extensions, getting my nails done or make up. The stripper lifestyle is not my kind of life. Sometimes, when I think bout giving lap dances or pretending to touch my pussy on stage, it makes me feel dirty- like a whore or something. I just lost my job at (EXCERPT DELETED) & started (EXCERT DELETED) today, & they're giving me free house fee/house mom fee for 30 days, so I'm giving myself one month of dancing (while looking for another job) and then I'll quit. Tom is going to pick me up around 11 to go look for jobs. I'm anxious/excited.

3) *Dating Dan. It's 5:30 AM so I'm not going to get too deep into this, but he drives me insane! He beat the shit out of me almost daily & talked to me like I was a dog. He controlled almost every aspect of my life, including the thousands I made dancing @ (EXCERPT DELETED). I'll never understand how he supposedly loves me and treated me like that. That's all I'll say.*

I went out to eat with Josh today! Danny found out (because I told him) that I'm in love w/Josh. I told him I wanted to be with Josh so badly & he told me that Josh feels the same way about me. I'm scared, but Danny is goin' to help me. He told me Josh has liked me if not loved me for like, 2 years. I don't know when it happened but I love Josh and want to be w/him ALL THE

TIME!
I'm helping Danny have a (heart) to (heart)
w/Chelsea about their relationship & their
son. Then bed time.

I (heart) Josh

I (heart)my mommy

I (heart) lots of people

(heart) Chelsie

I feel empty now. He asked me to
take his virginity. Told me countless times
that he loved me. We were going to get
married. I thought we were best friends.
Then he kissed me & I fell in love. I thought
he's been avoiding me because he knows I
don't approve of the dope, but it turns out (if
what Shannon said is true) that it was all a
lie. How could I be so stupid? I'm fucking
broken. He was/is my first non-selfish, pure,
true love.

WHAT THE FUCK.

I'M SAD AGAIN.

FUCK.

4

"He's taking two fat girls up the west end stairwell," Otis said over the phone during his Friday shift. Having made it home for the evening, I was taking it easy when Otis called from the desk to confirm that Robert Martinez was once again bringing prostitutes to the property when he was supposedly on business. "That piece of crap came to check in about ten seconds after I had just finished an under the table transaction with Bobo. Thought I was caught for a moment."

"You idiot!" I snapped, "You probably were!" I couldn't believe he'd actually go through with that sort of thing on a night that he was expecting Martinez to show up.

"Well, if you go now you should be able to catch him sneaking in his two ladies. Martinez is gonna be in 217, so you can literally watch them go in his door from the stairwell window."

"Perfect," I said with a fatigued sarcasm.

"Go!" Otis demanded as the volume of his voice increased, "Go now!" He sounded really enthused over my end of the deal.

Running down the stairs to the second floor and looking through the tiny window on the door that opens to the hall just to see my boss' boss with whomever he was cheating on his wife with that night didn't really sound all that worth it. But I'd be a liar to say I didn't hang up on Otis, grab my digital camera, and make for the stairway. There was something to be had!

Slowing down as I approached the door that separated the stairs from the hallway, I tried to be discrete to avoid being detected by Martinez in case he were within earshot. Dim artificial light against red brick momentarily removed my sense of depth perception as I felt the walls were moving in towards me. The scent of something foul hit me as I realized there must've been meat or food in the trash can. Coffee stains on the floor seemed highlighted, and for a moment I couldn't tell if the spatter on the wall was in fact coffee or blood. There was a tension that accompanied the seconds while I waited. Female laughter broke through the silence as they approached the door and finally came into sight.

Otis could be called a liar, though. He quoted me two fat girls with Martinez! Only one of the girls had any weight to her, while the other had the face of a hard drug user. They both looked to be in their mid-twenties, give or take. If they were going for trashy, they both dressed the parts well enough. The heavier girl grasped the necks of a single wine bottle in each hand. I wondered how much money went into this little party as I couldn't imagine any other motive for these two women to be here with Robert Martinez. With the flash turned off, I held my camera up to the window and snapped pictures for the ten seconds that I had the three of them within sight. The end result was about three solid pictures that confirmed it, as far as Otis and I were concerned.

Once Martinez had entered the room and the door to 217 had shut behind him, the elevator opened, and Bobo came into the hallway. Our eyes awkwardly met for a second as I quickly broke the contact and went down to the lobby to show Otis the fruits of our teamwork.

"So when should we blackmail him?" Otis inquired.

"Are you serious?" I asked as I recoiled with the camera.

"Well, yeah. What's the point of having the pictures if we're not gonna put 'em to use?"

"Leverage will be there when we need it! We use it when they've got our backs to the wall, or when we finally leave the ironically called 'hospitality' industry," I said. "I mean, if we tried to do it straight forward, we'd get torn down with him, no questions asked. To be anonymous," I continued, "is also next to impossible as they'd be able to identify the property based on the surroundings and room number hanging on the wall."

"I get it, man, but I've gotta admit, your approach is no fun," Otis said as a guest entered the lobby from the parking lot.

Leaving Otis to deal with the guest, I went back to my apartment to upload the photographs onto my company provided desktop computer. I also made two backups on separate portable flash drives to ensure that I would maintain the evidence. Putting them onto the company computer was dangerous as a handful of higher ups including Martinez had access to it at anytime through established computer links. Otis may claim that my approach is no fun, but having the off chance that Martinez may stumble upon the photographs himself was something I found exciting. It was career suicide, but I figured corporate, as incompetent as they were, had better things to do than go snooping to the depths where I hide anything not related to work. Part of me hoped that it would be found just to see how it would all be handled. Though I lacked formal direction, it would not complicate the process of protecting my own interests.

The weekend was lost in a haze. Martinez checked out on Saturday morning and left before Adam arrived, but not before making a reservation with me for the following weekend. With Otis working the following Friday's second shift, I was already planning a repeat of the previous evening. More blackmail equates to more leverage, and I was happy to be in the market.

A man of Spanish looking decent and

a woman named Rachel Vasquez, who was the person to register, checked in during my Sunday shift. With a standoffish demeanor, he seemed irritated that he even had to consider staying at this hotel. His head was bald and there was a teardrop tattooed under the corner of his left eye. Having never actually seen someone with such a defining tattoo, I kept my mouth shut as I registered the couple to room 220.

Adam arrived, and I only told him the half of the story where Martinez had gone dumpster diving and actually brought two ladies with him. I figured it would be best to keep news of my photographic endeavors below those in positions above myself.

"The part I find so difficult to believe is that he didn't want to talk while he was here at all," Adam said with a nervousness that's associated with hating your boss. "I got a quick email about some homemade *Wizard of Oz* motivational poster he wants me to put up in the break room. That's literally it."

"Might be a blessing in disguise; if he's just using our property as his doormat, there's little chance he'll later throw anything in your face," I suggested. "And what about the *Wizard of Oz*?"

Adam started to laugh as he spit out, "There's no disguise about it, man! It's pretty sweet not talking to him." He stopped laughing as he reiterated, "Personally, if he can make every stay at our property like this one, I might be happy working here."

"Well, he's coming back next Friday, so we'll see," I said.

"As long as he believes that I care about the job," Adam sighed. "You know, in total honesty, I hate my life."

Adam printed up four full color pictures of stills from the *Wizard of Oz*. The first was of the Scarecrow positioned to look like he were trying to think, the second was of the Tin Man holding the facial expression of tenderness and care, the third was of the Cowardly Lion pointing to the sky and appearing defiant and brave, while the fourth and final picture was a shot from behind the main characters as they approached the Emerald City. Above each of the pictures was a caption of words relating to the individual character. Above the Scarecrow it said, "We've got the brains." Above the Tin Man it said, "We've got the heart." The Cowardly Lion's caption read, "We've got the courage." And above the group shot it read, "To do wonderful things."

"This is so fucking hokey and stupid," Adam said as he looked upon what he had pinned to the wall of the break room.

I laughed and agreed, "Don't be too pessimistic about it, boss. Look, you've got your great staff in these characters here!" I pointed to each picture as it was appropriate, "Otis is a fucking idiot, Wolfgang is a heartless, cheating bastard, and I don't have any genitals!"

The rest of the weekend was relatively uneventful. College football was the only thing keeping business flowing as the cooler weather typically implied the start of the slow season. Our rates went up during the home game weekends which helped in curving the proportion of normal guests to scumbags.

I did have a guest threaten suicide on Monday morning. His name was Wesley Johnson, and he was a junkie who lived in a constant state of what he called recovery. On Sunday he came down to the lobby and asked if his father could pay by filling out the third party authorization form as he had done during a stay several months ago. This would all be well and good if it could have been done, but Mr. Johnson couldn't be bothered with such forms on the Sabbath. Wesley assured me that we would receive the forms Monday morning, and against my better judgment, I allowed him to stay, knowing that this would blow up in my face if not properly resolved. When he came in on Monday, he asked if the ritual of faxing and filling out forms could be postponed another day, to which I told him the opposite of what he wanted to hear.

Wesley fumbled around the property for another forty-five minutes before he came back into the lobby and sat in one of the lounge chairs while I dealt with a construction worker who wanted a room. After the construction guy left with his key, Wesley stood up quickly and came right up to the counter. With tears glazing over his eyes he said, "Could you call me an ambulance, please?"

Taking the request seriously, I responded with, "What should I tell them concerning an emergency?"

Wesley's eyes overflowed as tears streamed down his cheeks and turned in with the curve of his face. His expression contorted as he sobbed, "I don't want to live anymore. Please call 911 before I hurt myself!"

Enraged at the thought of this guy playing the victim, it was in total the fourth time I had seen him break down to tears in my lobby. All four of those occasions were over money. He'd bring up that he wanted to get sober, that he was looking into rehab. He preyed on and lived off of the empathy of others and I honestly only made the call because I was faced with it while working. Circumstances of the workplace would require withholding my actual opinions as I didn't care for this loser's troubles.

An ambulance did not come for Wesley. Instead, he was greeted by two police cruisers who spoke with him while he sobbed on the bench out front. He eventually left with the police. I checked him out of his room and filed him on the 'do not rent' list.

But that wouldn't be the end of it. Just after one in the afternoon, the housekeeper assigned to clean Wesley's room hurt herself due to his trash. As it turns out, Wesley threw his needles away without a cap. Anna, our housekeeper assigned to this trauma, emptied the room's trash can into her larger bag. When she went to lift the bag out of her cart during a laundry run, the bag bumped into her leg and the needle actually broke the skin on her calf.

Anna rushed into the lobby, sobbing and shaking, attempting to communicate what had just happened to her between chokes. Luckily, Adam was in the back office, heard the commotion, and did his job.

"Where's this needle?" Adam asked.

"In the trash bag on the floor, in the laundry room," Anna calmed down.

"You're gonna have to leave the rest of your board down. It's Tuesday, so it'll be slow. We're going to a specific clinic that will take care of you, and you're gonna be okay."

"Thank you," Anna said as she started to cry harder.

Adam went into the laundry room and secured the needle in a 'sharps' disposal container. After confirming that the leftover residue was not insulin, he asked Anna if she were ready to go. With tears in her eyes she nodded and expressed that she was calming down.

I Googled Wesley's name and address to find his previous mug shots. He had been arrested the previous year for deception to purchase drugs. I figure that translates to 'bought from an undercover.'

While they did leave in a rush, Adam maintained his sense of calm throughout.

Monday also brought Otis back into the mix. To this day I'm still not sure how Otis was able to negotiate getting weekends off. Seniority is the only way to explain it as he started six months before me. Opting out of the assistant manager position, Otis was the first pick for the same reason. But he had weekends off long before Adam said anything about promoting anyone. It actually used to piss me off back when I had a social life, but it's nothing to complain about anymore.

"You see the news?" Otis asked in a disgruntled tone. I figured he was just bummed about it being the start of his work week.

"What news?" I asked as he disappeared into the back. I left the front desk and asked him about it again as he clocked in for his shift.

"Lemme get online and I'll show you, man," he said as he went into the bathroom to change into his work uniform.

I was skeptical of whatever it was Otis wanted to share. Figuring it was some kind of partisan political article that equated to an attack ad or a rap battle music video involving fictitious portrayals of historical figures, I was ready to pretend that I cared. "What's this all about?" I asked with the skepticism hanging in my voice as he entered the front desk area.

Otis opened the internet and went to the website of the Columbus Dispatch before finding an article that reported the overdose of a young woman in her twenties, "Ronny sold her the shit," Otis finally said.

"You can't be serious? What was it? I thought Ronny was lying low for a while since getting in trouble. Didn't the philosophy involve selling pot and nothing else in order to remain unimportant? I mean, shit, his brother's in prison, and he almost got busted counterfeiting bills last year. What the fuck is wrong with him?" I questioned angrily to the poor choices our old friends were still making.

"Pretty sure it was heroin. Ron's been doing and selling whatever he pleases, man.

There's no stopping him until the law catches up. The thing is," Otis paused for dramatic effect as he lived to sensationalize any subject matter for the purposes of storytelling, "as you read on in the article, this poor girl is number seventy to die by overdose in the city this year."

"That sucks, man. Can't save people from themselves; it's sad," I said in an attempt to be comforting while being sure it came off as depressing. "So Ronny sold her the shit, huh? Did you know her?"

"Nah," Otis continued, "the article goes on to say that the drugs recovered from the scene were tested and have been found to be something other than straight heroin."

"So, the drugs aren't pure. Dumb asses that go that far should be well aware of the risks," I said as I flip-flopped from compassion to apathy.

"The chemicals were traced back to labs in Mexico, and the authorities have labeled it a death batch! It literally lulls you to sleep. Then it's over."

"Does Ronny know what he's selling to people?" I asked as I grasped the weight of the situation.

Otis nodded, "I saw the article last night and called him up. Ended up going over to his apartment to inform him face to face. He was pissed to have to take a loss, but I watched him flush the remaining junk he had."

"Did he even care about the girl who died?" I asked not really caring myself.

"As much as a drug dealer cares about

a junkie customer, yes. See, he got the batch a week ago, and instead of trying it himself, he just sold some into the market. Killed the first guy to purchase some, put the second in the hospital, and now Ronny has this Melissa girl's blood on his hands too. Trust me, he's not thrilled about any aspects of this round," Otis explained.

"Terrible," I muttered as I shook my head. "Gotta question."

"What's up?"

"You still buy weed from Ronny these days, right?" I asked.

"From time to time. He attracts too much attention from Big Brother, though. Between the feds chasing his actual brother across multiple state lines for drug related bullshit and, like you said, with Ronny getting caught last year counterfeiting bills, I try to keep my options open."

"Well, Penelope Rice and one of the other guys from 329 were pretty good friends with Ronny and his crew. Any word on Penelope?"

"Yeah, man. Meant to tell you but got caught off guard today by the news." Otis seemed relieved to change the subject, "I bought a bag Friday night after my shift. Bobo had come in twice last week on my watch which left me with enough for an eighth. So Jeremy Cross was there,"

"Fuck," I groaned, "what did he have to say?"

Otis cracked a smile at my reaction to the bringing up of Mr. Cross as he explained, "After throwing Penelope under the bus and being the informant that broke the camel's back on their whole operation, he said that she knew it was coming. That he only told me about it because of an argument between the two of them, and that she hitched a ride with some friends to an undisclosed location in Texas."

"Texas?" I was honestly puzzled, "We know anyone in Texas?"

"Not to my knowledge, man. It surprised me too!"

"Any freaks in today? Anyone I should be aware of?" Otis asked.

"Got a guest holding up in 220. Wolfgang checked the due outs today and was told that they didn't know whether or not they were going to stay. It's well past the latest checkout so,"

"So, they either need to pay or get the fuck out!" Otis cut me off.

"Looks like someone who wants to portray a bad ass. He's got one of those teardrop tattoos on his face."

"For real? That's fuckin' stupid. I mean, I've heard three or four different origins behind that ink. Not sure if he's been in prison for x amount of years or killed someone while incarcerated, but I just can't imagine getting that and attempting a normal life on the outside. What a freak!" Otis laughed. Getting serious, he changed his tone as he continued, "So, they're still holed up in there? It's three thirty, dude! Late checkout is one o'clock."

"I sent Wolfgang up to check on 'em about fifteen minutes before your shift. Hopefully, it'll be resolved soon. In the meantime, I'm gonna go to the store to get a few things. I'll see ya when I get back," I said as I turned to leave.

"Cool, man. See ya," Otis said as the desk phone started to ring. His tone changed to apathetic and mechanical as he regurgitated, "Front desk, this is Otis, how may I help you?"

With my car facing the Mexican restaurant, it was no more than fifteen steps away from the front entrance. As I opened the door to my 1999 Oldsmobile, the crash of shattering glass broke out behind me. I turned around to see the man with the teardrop tattoo had been slammed into the glass door by Wolfgang, and they were still grabbing and punching at each other. The glass of the front entrance door lay in pieces on the concrete below. Wolfgang pushed the man forward and through the frame of the door, taking the fight outside. Driving forward, Wolfgang pushed the man, and he fell backwards as a result of losing his balance at the drop of the curb. I watched as his head smacked onto the blacktop with Wolf crashing down on top of him. My friend yelled with the aggression of his accent, "Mutter fucker," a couple of times as he delivered three solid punches to the face, opposite side of the tattoo. He then stood up, spit on the man who was still on his back, and looked at me.

"What just happened?" I asked with my car door hanging open.

Wolfgang gave me a wave as Rachel Vasquez came through the shattered entryway.

"That fucker just committed assault!

That's what happened. You're gonna get fired!" Rachel taunted.

"Not true!" Wolfgang said. There was a fury in his eyes as he explained, "I come to door to see if check out or stay. This mutter fucker act like child and give me attitude. I ask you to leave when you no pay and he start running his mouth. I see him in lobby and had knife in hand. You know, he lucky I no kill him."

"He's right," Otis said as he came outside too, "Wolfgang knocked the knife out of his hand at the start. We've got that much on camera in there. Lady, get this guy into your car," he pointed at the other cars in the lot, "and get the fuck out of here before the police arrive."

And they did just that. The bloodied man got to his feet and walked away. They left in his car while eyeing Wolfgang as they drove off and out of sight. I feared that he'd be back to stir up more trouble or even try to kill Wolfgang, but he didn't seem the least bit concerned.

"Well, I'm gonna call Adam," I started, "so that he can get someone in here to replace the glass. Let him deal with it."

"Fucking handicapped," Wolfgang muttered. He then turned his attention away from the distance and said, "You know guys, sometime I feel like I want to just start killing the trash people that come through here."

"We all feel that way from time to time," I said as I started to call Adam from my cell.

Adam confirmed that he and Anna

were on their way back to the property-
Adam to take care of business and Anna to
get her car and go home for the day.

"What the fuck?" Adam yelled as he
approached the shattered remains of the
front door. There was literally a pile of glass
shards that were five or six inches high.
Anna had already started up her car at this
point. She was not the least interested, and
I couldn't blame her after a day like she had.
"First the guy threatens suicide, and we had
to get police here, then Anna gets pricked by
that stupid prick's needle and needed
medical attention, and now I get back from
the clinic to find the front door in pieces!
What the fuck is going on today?"

"What about some guy threatening
suicide and Anna getting pricked on a
needle?" Otis asked as I hadn't yet told him
about that part of the day.

"I'll tell you later, dick head," Adam
grumbled as he grabbed an oversized trash
bag and began cleaning up the broken glass.
Wolfgang and I helped Adam while Otis took
a reservation over the phone.

While we were down on our knees
scooping fistfuls of what looked like the
leftover meth from room 329, I asked,
"Doesn't get too much worse, does it?"

"Well," Adam started, "to me it does.
Today's the day that my wife and I revealed
that we've betrayed each other."

Shoveling glass into the plastic bag I
asked, "You mean cheating, or what?"

"Yeah, that sounds about right."

5

Wesley Johnson came back later that week. After calling 911 over his little meltdown and then having his exposed needle poke Anna, he was put on the 'do not rent' list and was no longer welcome to stay at the property. I had told him so when he called, but he insisted that he didn't need a room, that he just wanted to know whether or not we've had his car towed. I told him that his car was still in our parking lot, although I honestly had no idea.

When Wesley did show up an hour later, he started going through this Volvo that I assumed was his. He then stepped into the lobby with a new haircut and clear eyes. "Sorry about the other day, man," he said, "but that's the only way to do it where I can be sure they'll take me to rehab."

Nodding at the liar, I asked, "So you're in rehab?"

"Yeah, man," Wesley said smiling. "Hey, I've got a few more things I needta get outta my car, but I was wondering if you could call me a cab?"

"Sure," I nodded politely.

Wesley pulled a piece of paper out of his jacket pocket as he said, "This is the address where I'm going. Is it cool if I leave the keys to my car with you? My dad's gonna be here to pick it up tomorrow, and I trust you, Jessie."

"You really must," I said, surprised that this guy was actually considering leaving his car in my personal care for any period of time. "If you need to leave it here, that won't be a problem. We'll have the keys waiting for your dad. What's his name, by the way?"

"Larry Johnson," Wesley said.

"Thanks," I said as I wrote it onto a sticky note.

That guy actually left the keys to his new looking Volvo on the counter as he left in the taxi. If I were a little more impulsive, I'd take it for a joyride. Having the next day off made it all the more tempting.

After revealing that he and his wife had betrayed each other, Adam was back to his old habits of not being at work very much, maybe long enough to do the bank run. Adam would quickly wrap up the absolute minimum and go next door with Wolfgang for margaritas. When he did return to the hotel from the Mexican restaurant, you could smell the alcohol on his breath. It had come to replace his typical cologne as he struggled with the state of his marriage.

With the marital issues uniting with the heavy drinking, the burden was quite depressing to watch unfold. I had known for quite some time that things were bad at home, but it appeared as though the McCline family would no longer be putting on a charade for the sake of providing a normal family life for their two young sons.

"You just need to get laid," I said to Adam on Thursday.

"Fuck you, Jessie," he muttered back while leaning on the counter and exposing his face to the steam that elevated from his cup of coffee. "Wolfgang!" he said to the maintenance guy as he entered the lobby from the laundry room, "You and Jessie," he said as he pointed to the front door, "are fired. Get the fuck out!"

"You can no fire me! I am super genius number one!" Wolfgang declared with a caulking gun in his hand, "This place go to shit without me. You fired!"

Adam smirked as he said, "The guests have already let this place go to shit, you just make it functional and bearable for the lowest of standards."

Wolfgang would go on to defend his work, "If corporate buy materials I need, but they ignore us. Like we don't exist. Not my fault, dude."

"I'm just giving you shit, man," Adam snickered, "you really are what's holding this place together. It would be a hole in the ground in as little as two months without you around getting drunk and fucking fat women in the rooms."

Wolfgang laughed, "Hey, fuck you,

asshole! You no pay me enough so I need second job. That's why I bring sugar momma, and I respect you in that she always pay for room. And hey, what you do around here?"

"Just waiting to die," Adam said in a sullen honesty.

"Me too, man," Wolfgang said.

A black car then pulled in and parked under the overpass, and a middle-aged woman dressed in black stepped out into the parking lot. Motioning at her I said, "Why don't you hit on her? She's pretty hot."

"That's my wife!" Adam burst into laughter. It was the most genuine I had heard from him in quite a while. "Not a chance I'll be getting to sleep with her anytime soon!"

On that note we all laughed together.

Corporate came in the form of Robert Martinez, and Adam was fired from the Blue Moon Inn on Friday. I was to be left in charge of the property as interim manager until they could find a more experienced replacement. It was my day off of work, and while I haven't had much of a social life, I had escaped the property that day. With clear skies and the temperature in the sixties, it was a gorgeous day to be out, and there just happened to be a beautiful state park ten minutes north of the hotel. I had only discovered the place once I was promoted and actually drove that far to make the bank deposits. I wouldn't have even known that Adam had been terminated until the next day had he not called me, himself.

Surrounded by the bare branches of some nature trail, I remember listening to Johann Sebastian Bach's *Violin Concerto in A minor* on my mp3 player when I felt my cell phone vibrate. With Adam calling from his personal phone, I figured I had better answer it. I muted the music, removed the headphones, and took the call by flipping open my ancient phone and saying, "Hello?"

"Hey man," Adam started slowly.

"Hey, need me to work or something?" I asked.

Adam scoffed at my question before answering, "No, but since you're one of the crew, I figured I should be the one to tell you instead of one of those fuckers. I got fired today."

"What? Why?" I was genuinely surprised as corporate had typically taken an apathetic role concerning our existence.

"You know why, man. I've been a shitty boss."

"Yeah, I dunno, man," I started, "you may not have been around much lately. I get that you've got some troubles at home, but you stepped up when I found a dead body! You stepped up when we found out some trash was cooking meth in one of the rooms! You stepped up when Anna got pricked with a dirty needle, not to mention getting on your knees and cleaning up broken glass when Wolfgang and that angry guy shattered the front door!"

"I've also been stealing money from the company. They know it, Jessie, and that's the only part that they care about," Adam choked out.

"Holy shit. What?"

"Don't really wanna talk about it on the phone," Adam said as his voice returned to its typical calm.

"Got it."

"I'm also pretty sure they're gonna put you in charge until they can find somebody more qualified," Adam said.

"Fuck! You're kidding, right? Please tell me you're kidding!" I begged as I wanted no part in the general management responsibilities. "I already live there! I'm already on call twenty-four hours a day! I don't want this!"

Adam sighed, "I don't want this either, man."

"I'm sorry, Adam," I said as I realized how selfish I must've sounded, "we're gonna miss having you around. I'm just not sure I'm ready to be the head of the property."

"They'd rather put up with the loss of dealing with an inexperienced manager than to leave a proven thief in charge, but again, don't wanna talk about it on the phone," Adam explained.

The perfect temperature wouldn't stop me from overheating as the conversation ended and I came to find that I had broken a sweat. Dealing with Martinez and actually being solely responsible was far from what I wanted to do. Was Martinez planning to throw me under the bus after my interim service? Would I have to break out the big guns and take those photographs of him with the hookers as high up as I could reach? This turning point defined "terrible" as I, like most others, fear change.

As explained, I wouldn't have known about Adam's termination until my Saturday shift had he not called to tell me himself. Actually, I probably would've heard it from Otis, but at the end of the day Martinez didn't bother to contact me. It wasn't until I was working the desk the next day that the bastard confirmed anything at all. The shock of it all prevented our planned photo shoot as our nerves were shot and our feelings, complicated. I had one of the flash drives containing the pictures of Martinez with his ladies on hand in case things got messy, but it wasn't necessary as he was polite and stern without being a total jerk.

"Think you'd look more like management material if you got your hair cut." Martinez hinted.

"I would need to make at least ten an hour to consider it," I retorted, thus concluding that topic as most people in middle management want to concede as little ground as possible. I thought it wasn't too much to ask, but that was the end of the dialog concerning the length of my hair.

Two months was my sentence. I would be the interim general manager for the next two months while corporate determined who would be best to take over. Given permission to seemingly unlimited overtime, I took the terrible news with a grain of salt. I was also informed that it was believed I was doing a good job and would maintain the assistant manager on duty position upon the arrival of Adam's replacement as well as receive a pay raise that would exceed the economically capped two point five percent increases that usually equated to a pay cut when compared to the rate of inflation.

"It may not hit that solid number, ten an hour, but it will be significant."

Informing Samantha of Adam's termination and my new duties as she took over on the desk, I actually felt beaten and exhausted. She had already been informed by Adam the previous day and then at point blank asked me for a raise.

I half laughed and half scoffed at her, "I'll see what I can do, but for now I'm going to take a nap. Didn't sleep last night. Gonna do that now," I said as I walked away from Samantha and made my way to the stairwell.

"You do that. But for real," Sam insisted.

I turned around as I reached the doorway to the stairwell and shouted down the hall, "If they'll give me any sort of room to grant raises, you can trust that I'll go as big as I can get. I'm going to assume, though, that they'll hold off on that sort of thing until the replacement is here."

"But if they're giving you two months and I'm up for review in December..." Samantha trailed off.

"Like I said, if they let me do it, I will. If not, it may come late, but you'll be issued the back pay in the form of a really nice check."

Slowly, I took my sweet time going up the stairs that afternoon. That's when I remembered that since Adam had been fired, it was up to me to take the deposit to the bank. Turning around, I was sure to clock back in before taking the money and hopping in my car. At least it offered me the excuse to eat out. On the company's dollar and on the clock, I ate until I was full. Even with the crushing weight of newly appointed responsibility, I can't deny that I felt good.

After returning to the hotel, Samantha joked on my way in, "How's that raise coming along?" She smiled, and we laughed about it, but I knew she wasn't completely joking.

Reiterating that I would look into it, I assured her that the first email Martinez would receive from me would include the subject of respectable raises. I also then acknowledged that I would actually be going to sleep this time, as my work day was done.

After going up to the third floor, I had to use a key to access the concrete stairwell that took me to my apartment on the fourth story. It was at the top of those cold stairs in front of the door to my unit that I saw two severed fingers that were blue and purple with the bruising of early decay. Individually cut, they were positioned to look like the motioning of a 'peace' sign. The orange glow of undamaged nail polish highlighted the fingertips.

6

Calling the police should have been the only considerable option on the table. The orange tips brought images to mind of a strung out Penelope Rice as I assumed they had once belonged to her. Whoever had left the fingers in front of my door had intended for me to find them. That person also must've had a key to access the final flight of stairs to my apartment. The only other person I knew of with a set would've been Adam McCline.

I ended up calling Adam instead of the police.

"What do you want?" Adam answered with his typical response and tone that was saturated in apathy. It was said as though nothing had changed and honestly left me somewhat concerned.

Procrastinating on my response, I fumbled without articulating any real words.

It was an excellent start in breaking the ice.

"Jessie, what's up?" Adam asked with a tone that was no longer so careless.

"Know how you've got some things you don't wanna talk about on the phone?" I choked out.

Adam hesitated for a moment before responding with, "And still to this point, that is how I feel about that topic."

"I understand, Adam. Really. I've got something I don't really want to talk about over the phone. Wondering if you'd wanna meet for a drink sometime soon?" I asked.

"What the hell is going on?" Adam was blunt with expectations for an answer.

"You were the only other person with a set of keys to the flight of stairs that went from the third floor to my fourth floor apartment, right?"

"Yeah," Adam answered. His tone was a bit calmer as I had started communicating and not just rambling.

"Did you turn them in when you left yesterday?"

"Yes, I did," he answered.

"You give them to Martinez? What did he do with them?" I inquired with a sense of urgency. Proving to be poor at suppressing my emotions in a time of stress, I suddenly felt very foolish as I again failed to form an articulate sentence as I tried to continue.

"Jessie, what's going on?"

"Forget it," I said into the receiver while staring down at the peace sign on the bitter concrete. "It's not that important. I'm sorry I bothered you, actually. I'm gonna let you go," I tried to end the conversation while I still retained the perception of control.

"Wolfgang or Otis get a hold of them and take a shit on your doorstep, or what?" Adam was suddenly laughing as he chased his own imagination.

"I wish that were the case, man."

"Because that would be awesome!" Adam roared.

"Really, man, I wish one of those guys would've left actual shit on my doorstep and wrote derogatory comments on the door with it, but that's not what's really goin' on. Can we talk sometime soon, or what?" I restated myself to get the point across.

Adam continued to laugh before calming down and proposing, "How's Monday? The wife and I are talking divorce. She's already left with the kids, but we're going over some of the business tomorrow. I could meet tomorrow evening, but I think I'm just gonna stay at home and drink heavily by myself that night."

"Monday works. I'm on the desk and have to make the bank run once Otis gets in. I should be able to meet around four. Half past four at the latest," I said to specify the details.

"Four sounds good," Adam confirmed.

Leaving the fingers where I found them, I grabbed my digital camera and snapped two shots from an overhead position. These would not go on to be files on the company computer, as these were too high a risk. I put them on my private laptop. I wanted to keep track of something this invading in case the records would ever carry weight from which I could benefit.

Martinez must've put the keys somewhere that was accessible to everyone. I thought about it and wanted so badly for it all to be Martinez. Rat bastard was in some small town near Ann Arbor between the time that I last saw Penelope and the time that she disappeared. Wolfgang had talked about his desire to kill the trash that came through here. Otis was a misanthrope, who I'm pretty sure, hated the guests more than myself. If Adam could lie to his wife, what reason would he have to be honest with me? Cheryl was a loose cannon, I knew almost nothing about Abdul, and Samantha's sister used to run with some kind of Mexican gang. Then there's the housekeepers. I was overwhelmed and shaken by the plethora of people who could've done this. I wanted nothing more than to go back to bed and deny the day.

Enraged, I sat on the edge of my bed and seethed over the thought that someone was out to intimidate me through, what I considered a form of vigilante justice. I felt no pity for the death of a meth cook. "Good riddance to bad rubbish" was the line I thought of when considering to whom the fingers had belonged.

I felt that since the only other entity with access to the stairwell was the person who had decided to torture me, the best answer was to simply ignore the fingers. To walk past and pay them no mind would be the best way to excuse myself from dealing with it. Terrible; I know.

Lowering my standards, I actually

picked each finger from the frigid concrete and placed them into a single sandwich bag which I promptly threw into my personal trash can located under the kitchen sink. They were cold to the touch and stiff with rigor mortis. I wept, but I was pretty sure that it wasn't for Penelope. The fingers in the trash would be taken to the dumpster when I would naturally take it out to avoid being seen or doing anything that could be interpreted as suspicious. There was a menacing thought process to all of this, and I am pretty sure that with this action I have become subhuman. I am less than the scum to whom I rent rooms.

Feeling terrible, I'm still not sure why I didn't do anything rational. Fear is compressed to anger and once that moment passes, all that one is left with is action or the lack thereof. I lacked the will to do the right thing and contact the authorities out of my own paranoia. Were the fingers left there to intimidate me? Of course they were! I had already come to that conclusion! And in such a case, it could also be a threat. Someone has access to my home and could take me out if I reported this incident. My mind raced in circles as I searched for ways to excuse myself from taking responsibility.

Sleep didn't come easily. The smell of the fingers intensified as they seemed to cook in the garbage. It was about three in the morning on Sunday when I forced myself up. It was the first time out of bed that night to do something other than vomit. Irritated, I swung open the cabinet door releasing the heat of the trash that reminded me of the same sensation when touched with the overbearing temperature that came with finding the dead girl in 113. Feeling my stomach turn, I pulled the trash can out from under the sink and vomited on top of the filth. I then tied the bag shut, snatched it out of the can, and took it to the dumpster at the edge of the property. The sensation of that wretched heat remained upon my skin and within my nostrils until the bag left my hand, lingered in the air for a moment, and descended into the dumpster. It was at that exact moment that everything turned blue, and I felt the chill of the night air on my face. "What the fuck?" I whispered to myself. I could see the exhaust of my words as the bite of the air saturated my breath into a smoke-like fog. I suddenly felt alone and relieved to find a layer of frost had blanketed the grass next to the dumpster.

Sunday would be an easy day to work, as I honestly considered management duties to be less taxing than working the front desk as I didn't have to answer ringing phones all day. Something about the front lines of customer service left me terrified, and yet I had worked them for close to twelve solid years in one form or another. This was a new kind of problem, and I felt completely alone.

Having not gotten back to sleep, I clocked in at six that morning and immediately got to the bank run. Settling into the office, I checked the desk to find a number of keys that Adam must've returned. I went through each key individually and did not come to find a copy of the key to the stairwell that leads to my apartment. Deciding against my better judgment, I just went along with the routine of my job. With it being a Sunday, I would have to prepare the deposit in a night drop bag which also meant I couldn't make change, an inconvenience that routinely irritated me at the end of busy weekends.

The mandatory work was over before Samantha came in that morning as Abdul, our weekend nightshift guy, was cool with staying until eight to get in a couple of extra hours a week. Once the paperwork was taken care of, I started assisting in the housekeeping duties as Adam typically didn't schedule a head housekeeper on the weekends. I swept and mopped the areas that needed it before grabbing a cart and a trash bag to assist in stripping vacant rooms of garbage and soiled linen. I also assisted in laundry duties before our laundry person started her shift at two. I worked myself to fatigue while listening to metal as it was not a day for classical music.

Having been on the clock for twelve hours when I decided to crash out and get some sleep, I knew getting a case of beer would probably help me to stay down and actually get some rest. I ran out and got a twelve pack for dinner. Once I got home, it was only a matter of time before drinking three and a half bottles and passing out on the couch in the glow of the television.

Sleeping for more than ten hours is a pretty rare occasion, but it happened. I was out by seven thirty and slept straight through the night on the couch while I was bombarded with commercials and the horrors of regularly scheduled programming. I think I woke up sometime between five forty and six. It was the best ten hour stretch in recent memory.

I treated Monday like any other day shift. I awoke with perfect timing, made coffee, carried out ritualistic hygiene maintenance, took a shower, got dressed, drank coffee, grabbed my personal laptop, and made my daily descent into madness.

"If I'ma do you, I gotta do Jessie first," Cheryl said to Wolfgang as I emerged from the stairwell.

"Guten morgen, Mr. President," Wolfgang said as he saluted me.

"Morning sir, morning Cheryl," I greeted them.

"So, whaddaya say, Mr. President?" Cheryl insisted in keeping on with her previous conversation.

"To what?" I asked.

Cheryl looked me in the eye and said, "I told Wolfgang I would give him a massage if you agreed to get one first."

"No thanks," I responded.

"You sure?" Cheryl insisted, "I give a real good hand job. It'll make you feel alive, and the only way I'm gonna do Wolfgang is if I get to do you first."

"That's sexual harassment," I started, "and just to be clear, fuck that. No! What's wrong with you people?" I shouted.

They laughed at me as Wolfgang said, "Come on, dude! It'll be, how you say, cool."

"For real. We're not having this conversation," I said while shaking my head.

The day was particularly quiet on the desk. Martinez relieved me from having to sit through the conference call that week but insisted I get someone else to work the desk on Monday mornings. A couple of afternoon delights came in, and that's about it.

Otis arrived complaining about the work week, "Cheryl's gonna be late and shit. I shouldn't have to deal with it!"

"You're fifteen minutes late," I called him out.

"Yeah, but I'm talkin' close to an hour like, every night!"

Not having the time to care about Otis' fit, I ran the deposit to the bank and went to the Mexican restaurant where I met with Adam at the bar. He was sitting by himself and watching a soccer match with Spanish speaking commentators.

"What's up, shit head?" Adam asked casually before turning to look at me. "I'm just fuckin' with you. Grab a glass and I'll pour you a margarita," he said as he gestured for me take a seat.

"Thanks, man," I said as I accepted the drink.

"Let's get to business. It's almost four, and Wolfgang could show up anytime, but the closer it gets to five, the more likely it becomes," Adam said.

"What?" I was genuinely confused.

"The business. What do you want to talk about? How much I stole?" Adam asked defensively. I could see right through the calm front that he put forward. The man had reached a new low in discomfort. He had swallowed most of his glass and quickly poured another.

"No, no. I'm sorry that you lost your job, man. But I'm not interested in putting you on the spot," I said. "The whole shitting on my doorstep thing..." I trailed off.

"Something a little more?" Adam seemed puzzled.

"Something a lot more. I thought I was relatively liked at work."

Adam looked me in the eye and said, "Quit fucking with me, Jessie. What's going on?" He seemed agitated through the veil of a buzz he had gotten in before my arrival.

"Who do you think would be the most likely to actually hurt a guest?" I asked.

"I've got the best motive," Adam started, "what are you getting at?"

"I think someone hurt or killed a recent guest."

"No shit," Adam said with a smirk. He took another drink and motioned at me to continue.

"I've no idea who it was, to be honest," I said.

"So, what happened?"

"I think someone with access to room keys may have kidnapped or murdered a junkie."

"And some kind of evidence was left on your doorstep?" Adam inquired.

"Yes! Exactly," I was excited that Adam was following me.

"And why in the fuck are you telling me? You should've called the police immediately! Hell, for all you know I could be responsible for whatever was left on your doorstep," Adam talked down to me as he said this.

"Because I need to talk to someone!" I hissed before taking a long drink from my glass.

"That someone is a police officer. If you need to do anymore talking, you do it with a therapist," Adam paused. "Listen, man, I'm all for maintaining contact with you, and Wolf, and Otis, but if evidence of a crime was left on your doorstep, I'm not your guy. Don't accuse me, and don't try to get me to play fucking detective because you're too stupid to do the right thing. For some reason you feel sorry for my unemployed ass! Everyone with access to room keys is suspect, man. That means all of the desk clerks- especially the desk clerks! Housekeepers and maintenance get universal keys as well."

"Okay," I said as I opened my laptop, "you're the only other person who has seen this. Someone must've taken the key to the part of the stairwell that leads from the third floor to my apartment. Well, that someone went up to the top and left something next to my front door."

"I don't want to see this," Adam muttered in disdain.

"Come on, man," I insisted.

"If you do nothing but show me, we're both guilty by association. I'll be on your sinking ship if you show me and I do nothing. Fuck that, Jessie." Adam put up his open palms to express his desire for me to hold back as he reiterated, "Fuck that."

While I could tell that Adam was drunk, he stood by his convictions. "You really don't have any curiosity as to what it was?"

"Close the laptop," Adam ordered.

"What?"

"Just close the laptop and, tell me what it was so that I've got the chance to deny everything if it ever comes to it," Adam explained.

"You got it, man. Top me off, would ya?" I asked as I closed the computer and placed my glass within his proximity.

"So, what was it?" Adam finally asked as he refilled my cup.

"You remember when the DEA showed up and crashed that meth lab those fuck-ups were operating in 329? Remember how they didn't find the girl?"

Adam nodded, "Yeah, I remember they didn't find her."

"Well, someone," I lowered my voice, "someone else got to her first. They left two of her fingers on my doorstep. I know they're hers because I can vividly recall the bright orange nail polish," I explained.

"So, someone left human remains on your doorstep, you have pictures of it, and you're not going to the police? Had my wife been more like you, I may have opted to smack her around! Might've saved the marriage. Jesus, Jessie! You're a fucking idiot! Again, how do you know I didn't do this? Why tell me about it?" Adam slurred.

I played with the idea of a couple excuses before realizing that nothing would work. The truth finally came around as I admitted that, "I don't know."

"Let me see your phone," Adam

ordered.

"Why?" I asked, bewildered.

"I wanna make sure you're not recording the conversation."

"It's a shitty flip phone," I said as I handed it to him, "I think it may record a solid forty-five seconds. I'm not trying to deceive you here, man."

Adam pondered for a moment while his eyes searched the bar and scrutinized my phone. When he looked at me again, he finally said, "Let me see the pictures."

After witnessing the bright orange at the tips of the deep blue and purple stems reflecting in Adam's glasses, the photos seemed to sober him up as the look on his face suddenly became more collected. He stood erect, set forty dollars on the bar counter, and said, "Don't contact me again." He then walked out on me. He was truly disgusted or, at the very least, expressed it on the surface. Not only was I foolish, but I had made myself all the more vulnerable.

Drinking the rest of the margarita in the pitcher which was about two more solid glasses, I downed it fast enough to have stumbled out of there and back home before Wolfgang showed up, if he did at all.

Adam was right; I was an idiot. I realized that I had committed the second step in digging my own grave in that I informed someone else who could be willing to expose or further complicate matters. For all I knew, Adam never turned in the keys, and he left that girl's fingers on the top step. My mind raced back and forth over the possibilities that Adam was behind the digits left to rot on my doorstep. Difficult as it was, his words only stung until I drunkenly collapsed onto my bed. Hopefully, Adam's disgust was genuine, and he'll write it off as a waste of time. It would be even better if he were to have no memory of it at all. How I wished someone had just taken a shit on my doorstep.

7

The scenery was bewildering to the point of comfort. Blue skies with white obscurities that resembled clouds were limitless, unlike the path before me. Individual stepping stones were embedded into the grass of a field I found myself in. Sitting with crossed legs, my sense of peace and comfort took a humble backseat to a wanderlust that would indeed follow this path before me. As far as the eye could see, the path passed through a wall of trees and entered a forest of vast thickness.

I stood erect, stretched, and inhaled a sweetness that was the purest air I'd ever known. I found myself at the start of the stone pathway. Looking behind me, there were no other options when it came to direction. I could only bring myself to smile as the sun graced my naked body with a warmth that further stimulated my sense of comfort and peace.

Once in the forest, I could hear running waters in the distance. The trees were tall and healthy as I noticed there wasn't a single one that had fallen in this state of perfection.

While walking, a wolf approached with a warning. "Are you happy?" he asked.

I reached my hand out for him to smell as I replied, "Couldn't be happier."

He must've been a sheep in wolf's clothing, for he offered nothing more than friendly advice, "If that is the case, you shouldn't follow this manmade path. Stay here with me and we can play in the sun and rejoice for all of this, that which we have to be thankful for!"

I smiled and gave the wolf a pat on the head as I denied his request and expressed a desire to find whatever may be on the other end of said path.

Then came the warning as the wolf replied in a lower tone of voice, "Chasing after pipe dreams will result in unhappiness, my friend. I assure you, the desires of your heart will mislead you, just as this path will."

The desires of my heart layered a thickness over my skull as I smiled and told the wolf, "There must be a point to all of this. I must continue onward."

"I'll be waiting in the field if you happen to change your mind."

It was then that we parted.

After a short period of time, I approached a clearing in the trees where sunshine and tall grass lined the horizon. This opening was where the forest was divided by a river with a quiet current. The stepping stones allowed for a way to dryly cross the stream, and on the other side was my first reward- clothes. Halfway across the stream I heard a voice. Looking down, there was a fish on the stepping stone before me. He was pleading for help, "If I don't get back into the water, I'll surly drown!"

As though it were an instinct, I grabbed the fish and placed him gently into the river. He surfaced and thanked me.

"I'm glad to have been able to help," I replied.

"You're on the path, I take it?" the fish inquired.

"Indeed, I am."

"Abandon it," he said in a cheerful tone, "and swim with me. My friends are waiting upstream, but I assure you that this current will be much gentler than your current one."

I declined the fish's offer and wished him well.

Once reaching the other side of the stream, I embraced the waiting clothes by putting them onto my body. A single pair of blue jeans and a long sleeve flannel shirt excited me until they were on. For the first time since starting on the path, I felt weighted.

Admiring the beauty of the lush forest every step of the way, I couldn't help but to feel excited to see it come to an end. Standing on the edge of the forest, I could see the path continue onward into what appeared to be a suburban neighborhood that portrayed a sense of calm. It reminded me of where I had grown up.

As I made the first step that symbolized my exit, there was another voice, "Where are you going, friend?"

"I don't quite know," I replied as my eyes peered through the trees in search of the voice. "Are you hiding?" I asked while scratching my head in confusion.

"Not at all. You look through the trees, but are we not alive as well?"

I looked up to find a face on this great oak before me. In awe, a smile greater than any before it spread across my face. "Wow," was all I could bring myself to say.

"I know what you're thinking," she said, "but it is within your home that you'll find peace and happiness. This wanderlust has taken you down the wrong path, and I assure you, this forest is vast enough to keep you wandering the rest of your days. Please, stay here."

Her powers of persuasion were great, and yet I argued still, "But my instincts tell me..."

"Instincts lead animals astray all the time," she interrupted, "like a fish out of water or a wolf away from the pack; don't be fooled. Stay here, and I will nourish you with wisdom. There is much to explore. Even the trees reach out as we grow, but we never abandon our roots. I urge you to do the same."

Torn between my desires and the wisdom of the great oak, I was silent.

"I know your heart," she said. "You humans lack physical roots and therefore abandon them all the time. I personally find it to be disgusting, but as I am, you are not. Search for your heart's desire, but when you desire peace, I will be here. Remember, you will always be welcome."

I thanked the great oak for her wisdom and apologized for seemingly disregarding what she had told me. I bid her farewell and left the forest.

Without a clue, I followed the path on blind faith. The sun was still high in the sky, but there were street lamps that lined my path, and they were glowing, regardless.

There was an end to the path. From a distance I could see that it led right up to a social gathering. Well over a dozen people were seated in a circle of benches, conversing and laughing together. Curiosity took hold of my hand, and we approached.

There was Elyse, a girl that I had known long ago sitting there with her peers. I had loved her at one time. She was radiant, as the sun behind her hair created a halo effect as though she had stepped out of a Renaissance painting. Upon making eye contact, she flashed an inviting smile, and I took her hand in mine as though the years wouldn't pass as an acceptable distance.

Elyse introduced me around the circle, and her friends were quite friendly. They laughed at my jokes and accepted me as one of the group without hesitation. Laughter and smiles accompanied peace and comfort as they all replaced my wanderlust on the list of my priorities.

With her head on my shoulder, all physical sensation told me that this was real. I believed it too, right up until she said the words, "I love you."

A sense of urgency rose in my chest as I became fearful. Something was wrong and I could feel it in my heart. I tore my hand away from hers, sprung to my feet and shouted, "I can't do this anymore!" I ran away from the circle with a vigor that I had never known. What kind of wretchedness was this? Sadness accompanied isolation when I had finally stopped running. I had found myself in a field that separated suburbia from the trees.

Then it hit me; this was a dream.

It must be a dream. How else could any of it be explained? Over the past two and a half years, the only time I've seen Elyse has been in my dreams, and only in dreams can my heart compensate for its desires.

The setting sun told me to return to the forest. But the damage was done, and it was too late. I decided to confront Elyse and tell her of my conclusion. I could only hope to find her again.

I returned to the circle at the end of the path. Elyse's peers were not so welcoming this time around. "Why did you run off?" one of them asked. "You hurt her."

She wasn't there. I expressed my desire to see Elyse, and her friends took me to an apartment building. I knocked on the door numbered 417 and Elyse answered. With traceable tears in her eyes, all she could bring herself to say was, "Why?" before she buried her face in her hands and started to weep.

A machine gun rhythm pounded in my

chest as I worked up the courage to finally say the words, "I love you, Elyse." I put my hands on her shoulders and reveled in the touch. It was like facing a lie that you so desperately wanted to believe. "Elyse, I love you, but this is a dream, and I am going to wake up."

As I said the words, I awoke in my room. In disappointment I rolled onto my side and whispered her name. Closing my eyes again, I wondered why I was dreaming about a woman I had dated in college.

8

The next morning was a Tuesday and I was to work a desk shift. I was considering talking to Abdul to see if he'd be interested in picking up a desk shift or two so that I could focus more time and energy on the management aspects with which I had suddenly been burdened. He could pick up three solid shifts, if he wanted, which would put him at full time. I wouldn't bother him with it until his next scheduled shift on Friday night, but I was hoping that he'd be interested in forty hours a week plus benefits.

Watching Wolfgang pull up in Wesley Johnson's year old Volvo and park it in a different spot than the one where it had been left was a red flag cause for concern if I had ever seen one. It was the first time Wolfgang had been late without communicating it as long as I had worked there. Waiting for Wesley's father to pick up the car, it had been allotted a ridiculous amount of time to take up space in our parking lot as I was slowly coming to the conclusion that it had been abandoned. This too must've been Wolfgang's logic. Technically, my only option that would best protect Wolfgang as well as myself would be to have it towed immediately, if for no other reason than to get rid of the temptation to borrow this vehicle that made our cars look second rate. Any news of taking the car making it's way to corporate would cost someone their job as well as my own for allowing it to occur. At any rate, where was Wesley's family? Had his father even been informed that he was to pick up his son's car?

Wolfgang stepped out of the car, smiled, and gave me a wave as we made eye contact. I nodded and smirked to imply a vague approval of his blatant theft.

"You like mein new car?" Wolfgang laughed as he entered the lobby. "Tell me it's not cool!"

"Yeah, man, it's pretty sweet. I don't think anyone's coming to pick it up, to be honest. But hey," I changed tones to something more businesslike, "if you're going to turn that guy's car into something you're going to drive from time to time, don't let your coworkers see you taking it, okay? We could both get fired. I should just have it towed outta here."

Wolfgang nodded in agreement and said, "No problem, Mr. President! Only use it every now and then. Still use my own car most time. I park on far end of building from now on."

"Cool. If anyone asks me, I'll just say that we had to move it since it was taking up space close to the main entrance. We don't even have a contact number to reach this douche bag," I said.

"I no think anybody coming to get it, either. That's why I take," Wolfgang continued, "I had soccer game last night and my sugar momma love nice car. I only take now if boss say it's alright."

"I guess, man. I'll probably end up using it on a bank run if it's still here later this week. Make sure to leave the keys in the office in case someone does come for it. And hey, I've got coffee brewed in the back, you late piece of shit!"

"Oh, man! You sound just like Adam," Wolfgang laughed at me.

"Spent way too much time with that guy," I shrugged, "gonna miss having him around. I'm honestly scared of what corporate is gonna do. I mean, I know they've said they want me to hold down the place for two months and after that I'll be the assistant manager again, but what if they're holding out on firing me too?"

Wolfgang sighed, his eyes squinting to focus as he said, "Shit, you think they fire you too? If they do that, I no think I can handle new boss without you as bridge. I walk out and find new job if they make you leave."

"I appreciate it, but you've got a family to take care of," I said, knowing that Wolfgang wouldn't up and abandon the job for me if he didn't do so when they got rid of Adam.

After filling up his coffee cup, Wolfgang came back to the front desk and asked that I program his maintenance and housekeeping keys for the day. Using the Onity key machine to make them, Wolfgang autographed the log for signing them out before taking them and retiring for the majority of the morning to a vacant room where he would, more than likely, watch sports news.

Once Wolfgang had left, I spent the quiet morning getting the management duties out of the way so that when Otis arrived I could quickly wrap up and be done for the day. I prepared the bank run, batched out the credit card system for another business day, and replaced the security tapes that recorded the activities at the front desk.

As the day progressed and I wasted time on the internet, two articles caught my attention. They were both either comedies or tragedies, based on personal perspective.

The first I found as a direct result of Googling Wesley Johnson's name. It led me to believe that no one would be coming for the Volvo as he had passed away the day after he had left the keys with me. His obituary was vague, but I could only assume the worst as that worthless jerk-off told me he was heading back to rehab! I did find an article about him that explained he had been found with drug paraphernalia, and until the surfacing of the autopsy results, they believed he had overdosed. The same article and a dozen others made mention of the killer heroin mixture that had been retrieved from the scene. I wasn't sure whether or not the media was trying to sensationalize the surge in overdoses, or if they were telling the truth in that this specific batch was predominately lethal and linked to cartel based chemical plants in Mexico.

The second article reported a crime that had taken place over the weekend. Sylvia Bobo had been brutally murdered near her home by the casino on the west side of Columbus. Turns out that the investigators were stumped as what appeared to be a random act of violence would result in such desecration to the corpse. Bobo appeared to have been strangled to death, but an unreleased number of her teeth had also been removed after the fact. She had been reported missing on Friday when her children were left waiting for their mother at the daycare facility. Sylvia was found on Saturday less than an hour after the neighborhood organized search party had spread out to find her.

Not wanting to get Wolfgang's hopes up, I withheld Wesley's passing as it may be interpreted as his perfect excuse to get riskier in taking the Volvo. Figuring that the car would be repossessed any day now, I had all the more reason to keep it secure and on the property. I did end up showing him the article concerning Bobo's murder to gauge his reaction.

"Look at this!" I said as I pointed towards the monitor.

Wolfgang examined it for a moment in what appeared to be confusion, "What is this? Lady get killed over weekend?"

Clearing it up for him, I said, "It's Sylvia Bobo. She's been murdered, man."

Wolfgang's eyes widened before a smile broke out across his face. Once his teeth were showing, his mouth shaped to form the words, "Good. That kind of shit no need to be alive."

"Really?" I asked. "I mean, I didn't like the fact that she brought her prostituting here, but she wasn't the lowest of our offenders."

"Let me tell you, Jessie. Women all the same. They not normal in head. I know you and Otis take half money and give her room, but if she lived to find back to wall, she would spit venom like snake right into your eyes. They're evil, Jessie. All women the same," Wolfgang explained in his rant-like fashion.

Informing Otis of the Wesley Johnson overdose and the Sylvia Bobo murder upon his arrival at work, his demeanor shifted from the 'at work blues' to something that resembled the fulfillment of being thoroughly entertained.

"I think this is terrible in Bobo's case. Not even a prostitute deserves this kind of treatment," I said with the closest thing to remorse that I could express.

"Yeah," Otis seemed to agree, but for different reasons, "there goes our under the table operation. You know she's been paying for my weed for months now?"

Otis' honesty actually helped to break

the tension as I laughed, "You're a piece of shit, man. Whoever did it removed some of her teeth to make a necklace or something!"

"What? They took her teeth!" Otis yelled, "Without her, there is no trustworthy gravy train! Not to mention I think this whole management thing has gone to your head, Jessie. You sounded just like Adam, calling me a piece of shit."

"You and I have both spent way too much time here," I said as I clocked out.

"Tell me about it," Otis grumbled.

"Gravy train," I echoed as I cracked a smile.

"You think it was a disgruntled john?" Otis asked.

"You think it involved her business practices?"

Otis nodded, "Either that or she was randomly selected. The article say she was raped?"

"I didn't catch that in there, so probably not. Maybe it wasn't about the sex at that point. Maybe she robbed him on her way out or something like that."

"So, why take her teeth?" Otis shrugged as he couldn't understand what kind of motive would result in amateur dental work being performed on a cadaver. "That's just wrong."

Luckily for me, the bank run was a quick in and out that day. Exhausted and wanting to feel isolated without being at the hotel, I went to see a movie to get my mind off of things. I was able to kill two hours watching humans and different variations of aliens kill each other while discovering what it means to love. I'm not sure I had paid much attention, but the special effects were pretty enough to keep me distracted for a bit.

The theater itself was a discount place that had gone out of business, been sold off, and reopened three times in the past six years. I wasn't a big fan of the mall crowds, and I had been going to this little place in Westerville since I was a child. It had moving light displays that had been part of the foundation since the 1980's. It felt artificially futuristic and failed at creating the tacky illusion of taking me there. If anything about it were creepily mysterious, it would be that the tunnel effect created by the line of theater doors reminds me of the seemingly endless hallways of the hotel's second and third floors.

With the individual projection area feeling like a hotel room, I had the place to myself other than a teenage couple who happened to be more interested in each other's bodies than the movie. Had they been paying attention, they may've learned a thing or two about hormones and forced alien insemination and therefore have been smart enough to show a little restraint. I only threw Whoppers at them twice when they started getting out of hand.

Trapped with the idea that the movie was over, I had nowhere to go but back home. The Blue Moon Inn was the last place on Earth that I had wanted to be, and yet I really had nowhere else to go. I felt duped, and the worst part is that I did it to myself. How I wished I could trade places and be the careless teenager who went to horror movies as an excuse to hook up with a lady friend. There would be no compromise. I was Jessie Wilson; I was trapped.

On my return to the cage I had stopped and bought some coffee. Planning to stay up until the early hours of the morning, I would simply do the bank run the next day and be done with it as anything short of an emergency would automatically get a forty-eight hour window to respond by the standards established by the corporate office. I would do the minimum as Wednesday was supposed to be my scheduled day off.

I sat down at my desk chair, fired up the computer, and drew a gulp from my coffee cup before setting it down next to the monitor. The desktop had come out of hibernation pretty quickly, and I immediately jumped onto the internet. I hated myself for doing so, since I sat around online all day during desk shifts. To turn around, get home, and hop back on made no sense. Sometimes I'd find myself basking in the glow of the screen only to snap out of it and get some air.

But this evening was different. I ran through my routine of filtering through my various email accounts to see if I had anything that needed tending to. My first and oldest account with AOL had an email from my mother asking if I'd be able to get off work for either Thanksgiving or Christmas. Since I hadn't yet told her about Adam's termination, I ended up informing her that it would be the reason I would not be able to get away for the holidays. I had worked the desk on Thanksgiving and Christmas for the past three years in a row, and without Adam to adhere to our social contract that I'd get one of them off this year, I would be working a fourth. I apologized in advance for my holiday absence and said I'd give her a phone call soon.

After deleting the remaining junk from mailing lists I had signed up for many years ago, I moved on to the next account with Gmail to find a message from Elyse. Pausing as I stared blankly at the link, I hesitated and even thought about deleting it without further consideration. I was frightened or at least somewhat concerned that she would reach into her past and contact the failure that she had left behind. Those motives would be revealed upon reading it, but I wasn't sure whether or not I was up to such a challenge.

With temptation driving me to get rid of the message, I finally opened it and walked away from the humming computer. I then went to my stereo and started to play an Elton John album. *Rocket Man* opened the collection of greatest hits, and I would use Mr. John's music to comfort me in these times of awkwardness.

Having just dreamed of her the night before, I was suddenly frightened of what it meant. I had never been one to examine dreams or think that they meant anything other than basic psychological struggles with desire or guilt.

In the excitement of what kind of

subject Elyse's email could entail, I paced back and forth for a solid five minutes while the song filled the apartment. Hunger was disregarded as the moment left my stomach in knots. I found that I had broken into a sweat as I returned to the desk chair and brought my attention to the screen.

Elyse would be in town from the week of Thanksgiving and wouldn't be leaving to travel back to New York until after the New Year. She expressed that at some point during her time in town, she'd like to get a cup of coffee and catch up. With a short break from her research, Elyse had come home to spend the holidays with her family and unwind from the academic atmosphere. She even said that she felt badly for how we had to break it off but that she hoped I understood. Who was I to hold her back? As much as I had missed her, I too admired her. The final thing that the email communicated was an inquiry as to when I'd be available to get that coffee, which included her cell phone number that had since changed to a New York area code.

Out of an irrational fear of rejection, I would not give her a call. Knowing that Elyse had gone out of her way to contact me, I felt stupid in opting out of calling her cell, but I hid behind the veil of the screen as I replied by emailing her back. I gave her my cell phone number which hadn't changed since we were dating, and gave a few dates and times that I'd be available pending hotel emergencies are kept to a minimum. I specifically said that Friday afternoon would work out best for me as I had planned to sleep when I wasn't working on Wednesday, and Thursday was Thanksgiving, which I would be working and she would be with family. I felt strange as I sent my reply. It was as though I were making plans with a ghost. The glow of the screen warmed me as I wanted so desperately to equate that heat to her presence.

Elyse's follow-up email that I received forty-five minutes later informed me that Black Friday was perfect and wanted to know if I'd meet her at the Turkish coffee house near the campus. She claimed that she would accompany her mother on what she called a "fucking insane Black Friday expedition to Wal-Mart, the evil machine."

I was more than happy to go to that dumpy old place if that's where she wanted to go. The atmosphere was smoky and unkempt, but their coffee was great! When we had to pull study sessions, we'd turn the Turkish coffee house into a full day. We'd start with a regular concoction, cream, and sugar before moving forward and ordering a pot of their finest Turkish brew. You'd receive something the size of a teapot that was filled with their product, and two small cups the size of shot glasses. One of those glasses filled with the concoction from the teapot was enough to leave a person buzzing from the caffeine. The bottom of the shot glass would be layered in a thick tar like sludge with a grainy texture. It was bitter enough to induce a coma or possibly the polar opposite, something resembling the drug induced qualities of speed.

Elyse mattered to me more than the

other girls I've dated. After high school I spent three years going with the wind and from job to job. Both of my parents had worked in the home building industry, and they saw the bubble bursting years ahead of the curve. By the time the recession had hit, the both of them had lost their jobs. I too had lost my way as I went from dead end job to dead end job, using most of the money I made to fuel my constantly developing addiction to prescription pain killers. Running with the kind of people that I did, addiction was never restricted to a single source. Time was made to party hard as I snorted, smoked, and consumed my way through quite a number of drugs. Luckily, my list doesn't include heroin or meth, but it's still nothing to be proud of. Depression took grasp as it took drug abuse to feel normal.

That's when I met Elyse. She was two years younger than me and came from an upper middle class family that paid for her to spend the summer after her senior year of high school touring Europe. I was working at a coffee house when she returned to the States. I remember having taken a couple of Xanax that morning. Washing it down with two cups of coffee and two shots of espresso, I was happy and energetic, the perfect state of a routine worker. She came in, looked me in the eye, and admitted that she hated the taste of coffee, but wanted something sweet. Her brunette hair was cut to a bob which created the perfect frame for her face. She had hazel eyes and a smile that really touched me, though I would never admit it. Asking for a recommendation, I offered her a sugary latte whose taste hardly resembled the bitterness of regular coffee. I'm pretty sure it was some creamy pumpkin flavored cocktail of sugar and foam. My drug induced attitude resulted in her staring at me silently as I handed her the beverage. We held eye contact for a few more quiet seconds before she cracked a smile. Parting lips revealed the kind of teeth that shone with the beauty of the danger they represented when in a state of gnashing. Luckily for me, she happened to be smiling. Not another word was shared between us that day, but something clicked as she became a regular following our initial encounter.

A month after meeting her and tending to her lattes three or four times a week, she finally shared her name with me and asked if I'd want to hang out sometime. This broke a personal code, as I had adopted a philosophy of pursuit that read, "If the only environment you know them through is their place of employment, they're off limits." Maybe there was a solid gender bias in that I found her approach to not be deserving of the "creeper" label. It's a hypocrisy of which I was proud.

I had a roommate at the time. We shared most everything including addiction. Sometimes we weren't always on the same team, meaning he and I would hold out if we were short on supply of whatever we happened to be abusing at that time. His overdose and passing brought forth the typical fork in the road that those sort of situations bring up, and after falling on my face a few more times, I tried to kill myself. I decided suicide was the best of my options. The bottom felt like honesty as I knew hope was out of reach. I was in too deep, and doubt consumed any and all attempts at recovering. I got one last glass of water and went to my bedroom. Drinking only a third of the glass, I set it down on my nightstand as I removed my belt. I then placed my desk chair next to the door. Creating a loop with the belt as though it were going around the waist of a malnourished ghost, I closed my bedroom door onto the end of it, effectively creating my makeshift noose. Placing my head into the loop, I tightened it around my throat, inhaled deeply, and held my breath. Exhaling slowly, I kicked the chair out from under my feet, blacked out, and woke up on the floor to find that the belt itself had snapped.

In my defeat and further shame, I called Elyse and explained to her the entirety of my addiction to my failed suicide attempt. Such selfishness was met with care as Elyse did something unexpected; she cried. She wept in the face of my struggle, and her expression left me feeling an awkward comfort. It was the first time that I had actually felt loved.

I got my life together and got sober. She happened to be there when I emerged from the hole. Because of her, I went to college and used her in a way to hold myself accountable. I had dug myself out of the bottom and gazed upon a potential in which I had long since stopped believing, a potential that I could identify as my own, a life worth living.

Elyse left. There's not much to say about it. I had gone to get educated about the things I happened to be interested in, and while she was no less interested, she was much more goal oriented in that she sought to be a college level professor and would stop at nothing to make that dream her reality. After getting through the history program at Ohio State, her choice came down to a full ride at New York University or our relationship. While it still hurts to think about it, she made the better choice.

After she left I took up drinking and smoking the occasional joint again but have remained disciplined in not seeking out the overly self-destructive tendencies I had once embraced. Elyse may have helped me when I needed it, but while she may have been the one to have gotten the ball rolling, her departure would not trigger deviation from my personal responsibility to remain sober. I stood on my own. How this denial reminds me of that prostitute's diary where she denied being a junkie! What harm is a few drinks from time to time?

Now she wanted to meet for coffee. After being gone for two and a half years, she wanted to catch up. The resentful child in me wanted to piss at her offer in the most ruthless way that I could imagine. To leave the past behind was the option that I was greedily considering. The maturity of this desperate and lonely man I had become was preparing to jump at the opportunity to say "hello" and simply be in her presence, if only for a moment. While I longed for human contact, Elyse was someone whom I valued more than your average person. Romance was not my priority, although I would not deny a holiday rendezvous. Was maturity erased at the acknowledgement of being desperate? If I give the situation a middle ground approach, I should be able to come off as normal, or stable, or not dealing with the failure of having the hotel define me. She wanted to meet for coffee, and my heart raced as I decided to oblige.

Thanksgiving was much like Christmas in that I routinely worked an eight hour shift while the boss took the day off to celebrate with family. Last year Adam and I had worked out a social contract that I would be getting Thanksgiving off this year to visit my family. With his departure went my holiday as I found myself earning time and a half on another dead Thanksgiving shift.

Other than the depressing regulars who were stranded at the Blue Moon, the shift was barren in terms of business. I screwed around online and couldn't escape the anticipation of seeing Elyse for the first time in over two years.

Remembering shifts of Thanksgivings past, I did something my first year working the holiday that should've resulted in me losing the job. Adam was out of town with family and wouldn't be back until Saturday, literally leaving Otis and I in charge of the place. This wasn't out of the ordinary as Adam was an elusive manager. I was editing a mediocre report on what kind of ego it took to invade Russia during the winter when a towering burly man strolled into the lobby. I could smell him the moment he walked in, and he looked as though he hadn't showered in some time. With hair as long as my own and a thick red beard crusted with filth, I assumed that he didn't have the kind of money to get a room. He wore a tattered hooded sweatshirt at a temperature that demanded a full jacket. After admitting he was homeless, he asked to use the restroom. Once he was out of there, I gave him the ham sandwich I had brought with me for lunch. With tears forming in his eyes, he took the sandwich baggy into his blackened hands and thanked me. The tips of his finger nails were caked with dirt and the filth around his eyes ran like mascara as he wept. I watched him as he left the lobby and entered the side door at the end of the building.

Later in that shift, I went upstairs to check on some rooms at the end of the hallway to see whether or not they had been cleaned. Instead of making a housekeeping key, I made three individual keys on purpose. I had a hunch I'd run into the homeless guy loitering as he tried to stay out of the cold.

When I got to the end of the hall I found him sitting in the corner with the empty sandwich baggy on the floor next to him. He looked disappointed in making eye contact as he assumed I'd be asking him to leave.

"Hey, man," he said as he gave me a nod.

"Hey there. Hold on a sec, I've gotta

check on something."

"Okay," he responded with dwindling faith that lightning would strike twice and I'd again be friendly to him.

Checking the three rooms at the end of that hallway to make sure that they were clean, I had strategically made the individual room keys hoping that I'd run into this guy. "Hey, man, I wanna talk to you for a minute," I said as I shut the last door behind me.

"It's cool, man. I'll be on my way," said the homeless guy who refused to make eye contact.

"That's not what I said, man. What's your name?" I asked.

"Really? Um," he paused as though no one had asked him that question since he had last showered, "Randy. It's Randy Riggs."

"Well, my name is Jessie. Here's the deal, Mr. Riggs," I started, "my boss is outta town for the holiday and I can put a room down as out of order for twenty-four hours, no questions asked. I'm gonna give you this key and you can sleep, catch a shower, and stay out of the cold for the night."

His eyes swelled and overran in a manner that made his response to the sandwich appear minimal, "For real? Thank you, man. It's so hard anymore. Once you get to a point where you look like I do, you're less than human! Nobody has treated me with kindness in so long. Thank you, thank you," Randy said as he hugged me. I didn't mind the smell as this grateful man was truly overjoyed by this small gesture.

"There's a catch," I said to spoil the moment. "My boss will be back and this is a business. If he finds out that I'm giving out rooms for free, it's my ass that's on the line. You've gotta bail by noon tomorrow or you're putting me in a bad place. Got it?"

With tears streaming down his face and into his beard, he shook his head as he cried and said, "No problem, man. I got it."

"Cool. Take care, Randy. If you don't mind, I may pop by your room later with some kind of makeshift meal."

"Thank you," Randy repeated.

"You're welcome. But I'm serious," I deepened my tone to imply that I meant what I was saying, "you need to bail no later than noon tomorrow. I'm happy to help you out, but I'm counting on you."

Randy was trapped in a loop as he again said, "Thank you."

Give them an inch, and they'll take a mile. While I had the following day off of work, Randy holed up in the room and didn't leave on his own free will. He went unnoticed for an entire second day, and it wasn't until Cheryl's third shift Friday night that anyone took notice of the unaccounted man staying in room 338.

You wouldn't believe the balls on Cheryl. She made a key to the room and went up there in the middle of the night. When she went to open the door, it stopped about an inch or so in due to the security latch. Yelling into the room, Cheryl got no response but knew all the same that someone was holding out. I can still remember her story as she described throwing all two hundred plus pounds of herself into the door, breaking off the security latch. After forcing her way in, she grabbed Randy by the ear and forced him to leave while badmouthing him the entire way out.

Figuring I had lost my job, the only thing Adam said on the topic was a sarcastic, "So, I hear this place gives free rooms to homeless people, now." He then followed it up on a serious note in saying, "I understand your heart was in the right place, but ninety-nine percent of the time they will turn around and throw you under the bus just like this guy did. Every sob story that wins you over will burn you in the end," Adam sighed as he shook his head and said, "don't give out free rooms anymore, fucker."

Other than the under the table operation with the now deceased Bobo, I had not given a free room to anyone not related by blood since then.

This Thanksgiving was no different in that it was dead like the other time and a half holidays. It was so quiet that after the checkout time had passed, I sat back in the office and put my feet up on the desk. I think I saw Wolfgang take off in the Volvo, but I can't clearly remember. From there I answered the phone once to answer the question of a housekeeper as to whether or not room 226 was staying over or checking out. Beyond that I dozed off in the office and didn't wake up until Otis arrived for his shift at three.

"What the shit? For real?" Otis laughed, "Wake up, ya bastard!"

Stirring from my sleep, I stretched and greeted him, "What's up, man? It's gonna be a slow one for you."

"Good," Otis' expression was drenched in sarcasm, "I don't wanna do anything today anyway. How great it is to waste another holiday here, huh?"

"My sentiments exactly, man. Adam promised me Thanksgiving off this year, but here I am."

"He promised me Christmas off, but that doesn't look like it's going to happen now," Otis complained.

I shrugged as I went into manager mode, "Samantha doesn't celebrate Christmas. If you want, I'll ask her real nicely to cover for you. I'll work the morning as planned and you can spend the day with your family."

Otis recoiled and shot me a look of disbelief, "Really?"

"Yeah, man. In my position, I'd hope you'd do the same for me," I explained.

"That's awesome, man. Thanks!" Otis said in a tone that reminded me of Randy Riggs.

"Relax, Otis. It's not that big a deal," I suggested.

9

Black Friday is another dead holiday in the hospitality industry as our service based economy takes a back seat to manufactured goods from far away. True patriots are out looking for the best deals while only a handful of cheaters and regulars make their way to the Blue Moon. It was almost nice to work the holidays as they were moderately uneventful.

Von Hertz showed up that day, actually checked in during my shift. He appeared worn out and weary as he initialed the registration card in the strange way that he had become accustomed to over the years. Simply writing the first letter of his first name and circling it, I had witnessed Von Hertz legally make his mark. I noticed that he carried a small backpack, but it wasn't my business to question it.

"Hey, man, what's happening?" I

asked casually as I folded his reg card and placed it under the counter.

"Not much. Family thinks I'm out shopping. I'm gonna take it easy for a while, maybe pick up a few things on the way home," Von Hertz said cautiously, his voice dedicated to making the small talk as short as possible. He was a thin man with a crew cut. With the face of an average Joe, Von Hertz would be much less of a shambling target if he just carried himself a little better. Handing Von Hertz the key to room 323, I nodded to acknowledge his body language and let him go. He then painstakingly handed me a fifty dollar bill and quietly muttered, "For movies."

"Got it," I said as I entered his fifty dollar deposit into the system and turned on the movie options for his room. The elevator opened for him before I spoke again, "And hey, Von Hertz,"

"What's up, man?"

"We're not exactly sure what you're thinking or doing up there. It's none of our business, really. But we're not bugging the room. You don't have to worry yourself into a frenzy and unplug everything in there. We're not Big Brother. When you close the door to your room behind you, you are as close to alone as you're gonna get without going someplace that's built to be soundproof," I explained, not sure as to why I would seek such dialogue with him.

Von Hertz stared at me while the elevator closed. It seemed to strain him as he returned with a drawn out and slurred, "Thanks." He then pressed the elevator button again. It opened immediately as it was still on the ground level and he vanished into it.

As the door closed he said, "Four one seven zero two."

The bastard must've watched me program his key and now knows my code. Luckily, Adam had trained me on reprogramming individual codes for the Onity machine, and I would be able to create a new code for myself while voiding the old one. It was still a bullshit hassle I could've done without.

"That piece of shit watch you to get your key code? That's fucked." Wolfgang was pissed off when I told him about my encounter with Von Hertz, and he ranted to express it as he boasted, "In mein home country, we call him 'bitch' and kick his ass in street."

"It's cool, I've got a new code now, and the old one isn't going to work," I explained.

Wolfgang looked around before lowering his voice and saying, "You know, sometimes I wish mein Führer would come back. World need people like him to make world better place."

"Hitler?" I smiled to mask my disgust.

Wolfgang gave a Nazi salute as he said, "Yes sir! Hitler get rid of this jerk-off trash."

"I don't think he'll be coming around too much longer," I said.

"Good, good," he approved.

"Hey, Wolfgang, I gotta question for ya. You taking the Volvo out tonight?" I asked.

"Why? You need, Mr. President?" Wolfgang laughed, "You going to meet with lady and need nice car, huh?"

"Yeah," I nodded, "going to meet for coffee."

"For coffee?" Wolfgang sneered, "Why you no drink alcohol? Every lady like alcohol."

"We might have some drinks later, but we've known each other a long time, and it'll be easier to catch up if I'm not buzzing," I explained.

"Elyse back in town? I can read on your face," Wolfgang nodded, "and when you say that you two know each other long time, am I right?"

"Yeah, man. She's in town for the holidays," I answered honestly.

"Nice!" Wolfgang was enthusiastic about it as he went on, "Elyse very sexy. Very good, man. You have fun, and take Volvo! I no need car tonight. I just take husky to dog park this evening."

"Thank you, sir," I said.

"No problem, Mr. President," Wolfgang replied as he handed me the keys.

Pulling up to the parking lot of the Third World Coffee and Hookah Lounge, Elyse was waiting for me in a car across the lot. As soon as I stopped the Volvo, I watched her step out of a blue 2002 Ford Focus that had seen better days. I knew it was her car when I pulled up. She's had that thing forever! She probably left it with her family while using the mass transit system in New York.

The layers that she wore to protect against the weather would not conceal a shape that still appealed to me. She wore a jacket that outlined the curves of her frame, and I would conceal my lust. I was just simply looking for a friend.

Elyse waved at me as I stepped out of the Volvo. "Hey there!" I waved back and started walking towards her in the parking lot.

She started walking towards me as she spoke, "Jessie! How are you?" Then she was taken aback as she said, "How new is that car?"

"It's a 2011," I said while failing to keep it cool. I was bad at being deceitful.

"How could you afford something like that?" Elyse pointed at the Volvo, "You move on up in the world, huh? I thought in the email you said that you still worked for the hotel."

"I do." I tried to jump through the hoops. "I'm the assistant manager now."

"Adam finally manned up and gave you a promotion, huh? You still wouldn't make enough to afford that thing," Elyse said as her breath turned to fog in the chill of the air.

I foolishly stumbled over my words before compromising in the form of a half truth, "It belongs to a guest from work. Let me borrow it too..." I tripped over my words again and trailed off.

"Let you borrow it to impress a girl? Not impressed," A cross armed Elyse bluntly stated in the setting sun. "We've known each other for too long. We're past that part where you should feel the social pressure to impress me. You actually borrow the car of a guest at the hotel?"

In my shallow guilt, I nodded to confirm her accusation and to show that I agreed and felt quite stupid. "I'm sorry, this is a terrible way to break the ice," I said with a vulnerable wavering in my voice.

"It's okay, Jessie. You ready to get our Turkish coffee on?" Elyse said as she finally shed the thick skin and broke a smile.

Once inside we removed our jackets and adjusted to the heat of the atmosphere in a hookah lounge. The place had hardly changed besides the replacement of furniture. The lighting was dim and the colors were dark as they ever were. Hardwood floors were scuffed with years of travel, and a smoky haze floated towards the ceiling that reminded me of previous nights spent there. The removal of her jacket and hood reaffirmed my suspicion that she still looked great. As long as the pursuit of higher education hadn't watered her down to socially awkward, she'd be considered far out of my league. Reminding myself to practice a gentlemanly philosophy was increasingly difficult as we ordered a pot of Turkish coffee and took our seats.

"What kind of hookah do you want?" Elyse asked.

"I'm not sure. It's been a while. They still slice a fresh orange and put it in the water when you order orange flavored tobacco?" I asked.

"I've been in New York for most of the past two and a half years. The only time I've been home between then and now I've had important matters that included not straying from my research."

"Figured this was always the best place to get our study on, ya know?"

"Maybe it was then, but my habits have changed drastically. I've got a different approach these days, and it includes a much more stable and peaceful atmosphere."

"Touché." I laughed before making a suggestion, "How about we mix apple and strawberry?"

"That does sound pretty good," Elyse said as her eyes scanned the menu for something better suited to her tastes. "What about blackberry?"

"You want blackberry?" I inquired to move that option forward.

"Yes. Let's get a blackberry flavored hookah tonight!" Elyse declared.

While making the order, I noticed that the clerk was an Ethiopian man named Alem who had worked there many years before. He had been living in the states for at least the past ten years that I've known of him as the business owner of the Third World Coffee and Hookah Lounge. He was a tall and dark man with a head that he consistently kept bald. We made eye contact, and he recognized me as well.

"It's good to see you, Jessie. How are you?" Alem asked.

"Nice to see you too, sir. I'm doing well," I replied. "How's business?"

Alem nodded as he said, "It's not bad at all." He then casually changed the subject, "Are you with the girl who ordered the Turkish coffee?"

"Yeah. You don't remember Elyse?" I asked.

"You're kidding?" Alem seemed confused.

"Her appearance hasn't changed very much," I pointed out.

"I see her now. Pretty embarrassing. I feel foolish, man. Let me give you a hookah on the house."

"Thank you, but that's really not necessary," I said.

"I insist. Not only do I insist, but I won't hear an argument in my establishment, sir," Alem said with a smile. "How's Daniel these days? You ever hear from him?"

"There's a name I haven't heard in a while," I said as I was taken aback. "Lost contact with Dan when he moved to Chicago on a whim. He's been off the radar ever since, as far as I've checked."

"Damn. Well if you see that cat, you tell him I said 'hello,'" Alem nodded his head at the thought of our old friend in Chicago.

"You got it, man."

"You guys doing business or what?" an impatient voice asked from behind me.

Alem scoffed at the kid behind me, "You can either wait or leave. It's up to you, but do not rush the person in front of you as it shows disrespect to myself as well as the gentleman before you."

"Sorry," I cautiously said as I moved forward with my order, "could I get a blackberry hookah?"

"You got it. Anything else?" Alem

asked.

"If it's not too much, an hour after the Turkish coffee, we'll need two glasses of your finest hot tea. It really is the best I've ever had."

"Two hot teas in sixty minutes. Check. Got it, man," Alem said to move the transaction forward.

Taking a seat in the front part of the lounge put Elyse and me in the window that's visible to those passing by. It was an interesting place to kick back and smoke.

Elyse was the first to speak as she observed, "Typically, everyone that walks past the window that sees people smoking ends up doing a double take."

A tall single hose hookah with shimmering silver hardware and dark blue colored glass was brought out to us by a young girl who appeared to be a college student, based on her sweatshirt. When we first started coming to the Third World Coffee and Hookah Lounge, it was primarily run by Alem and members of his extended family, but as their lives had been reshaped in America, Alem had taken to hiring local college students. It would be another five minutes before our Turkish coffee would be brought to us, but Elyse wasted no time as she applied the plastic mouthpiece over the tip of the hose and drew smoke from it.

"Wonderful! It's been a long time," Elyse said as she exhaled very little actual smoke. "Takes a bit to get it rolling," she observed and then explained, "Lemme try that once more," as she again drew from the hose. Her eyes widened at the peak of the inhale. In releasing, her words were accompanied by a thick cloud as she spoke, "There we go!" Passing the hose my way, she gave me a nod as she asked, "How are you these days, Jessie?"

Tasting the blackberry flavored tobacco, I let go of the smoke in my lungs and answered, "Things have been so-so as of late. Work has been complicated as the dick heads in corporate fired Adam a couple of weeks back. I'm in charge until mid January or whenever they can get a replacement to fill the void."

"Oh, shit, you're in charge? Sounds dangerous," Elyse laughed as she speculated.

"Yeah," I started before hitting the hookah again, "it's actually pretty rocky right now. Since getting promoted to the assistant manager position last February, I've actually moved into the hotel. There's a full single bedroom apartment unit on the fourth floor that's been my home since then."

"That's weird. The place is creepy enough; I can't imagine living there. How's Otis? You two still running the show together and getting into crazy shit?" Elyse asked as I passed her the hose.

Laughing, I said, "He's the same old sensational misanthrope. Working customer service and refusing to find another job, all the while still making up conspiracy theories revolving around Cheryl giving hand jobs to regulars."

Elyse rolled her eyes as she asked, "So who actually let you borrow their new Volvo? Your guests have never seemed to be in their right minds, but really, who lets the clerk at some dumpy motel take their seemingly brand new car out for a night on the town?"

"It's actually no big deal," I responded while trying too hard to be cool.

"If you're not insured to drive it, it's a big deal, you smart ass. Answer the question!" Elyse continued with her relentless pursuit.

When presenting something you'd rather not, it's best to conceal the truth in the verbal arena of sarcasm. With established eye contact I said, "The owner's dead. Some junkie had his daddy pay for it, abandons it in our parking lot while leaving me with the keys. He overdosed the following weekend. No one has come to take it, and I figured the rightful owner is probably busy with ritualistic shopping or social isolation, depending on how he feels about the biggest shopping day of the year."

Elyse laughed before confronting me, "I could always see through you when you tried to play something off. What you're trying to pass off as a comical lie is actually the way things are. Am I right?"

My good mood was momentarily shot as I mechanically churned out the word, "Yes."

"Jessie, what else is the matter?" Elyse asked with the weight of concern in her voice.

"It's just work related stress. Since moving onto the property, my whole life has been work. I'd really rather talk about something else." I said as Alem brought out a trey that presented two clay cups that were each the size of a shot glass and a pot that contained the Turkish poison of our choosing. "Thank you, sir," I said to Alem.

"You're both very welcome. I'll have two glasses of our finest tea ready for you in an hour. If you come to find that you're in need of anything else, don't hesitate to let me know," Alem finished speaking by giving us a nod and turning to walk away.

"Work related stress has never forced you to steal a car," Elyse quickly returned to the subject at hand.

"Enough time at the Blue Moon and you'd compromise all of your morals away," I said as I filled our cups with the Turkish sludge. "I'm not proud, but I'm also not too worried about it. Think of it as a one-time flub, my dumb ass trying to impress a girl with some lost and found items from work," I tried to shrug it off and absolve myself of any responsibility.

"Trying to impress this girl," Elyse said as she jabbed at her own chest, "doesn't justify stealing a dead man's car. Work related stress doesn't justify stealing a dead man's car. There's something you're not telling me," she rationalized. She demanded an explanation but was not angry.

"There's a bad batch of drugs going through the market. It's so far from pure that some of the extra chemical mixture is traced back to cartel operated plants in Mexico. It's killing people, and we've been finding them in rooms on occasion. It's just difficult to walk into a room expecting to clean it, hoping that it's not trashed, only to find some dead kid. It's been happening enough to weigh on me," I explained my half truth coldly. "Kinda shit gets to you after a while."

"Why do you still work that shit-hole hotel?" she stressed her words.

"I'm a glutton for punishment," I cheerfully admitted as I leaned back into the cushioned corner of the sitting structure that circled the area in front of the window. "But we didn't get together to talk about my job. How's life? How's school treatin' ya?"

"Research is crazy, but I needed to take a break, come home and stretch. Gonna end up spending at least half of my time here studying and staying on top of my research anyway, but it's just nice to come home every once in a while. Much like your job, I'm not up for talking about it this evening. Maybe another time," Elyse said as she passed the hose back to me.

"Works for me, although I'd love to hear about your research, if you ever feel like sharing," I said before hitting the hookah.

"One serious question, and I'm sorry to ask this," Elyse started to speak as I passed the hose back to her. She grabbed and held my hand as she spoke, "I just wanna make sure you're doing okay these days. I've gotta know; you've been staying clean, right?"

"Do I look that bad?" I asked in genuine confusion. "I may have partied hard when I was carefree and in high school. I may have dabbled a bit here and there in college. These days I may drink a little more than I should. I might get my hands on some pot once a month or so. I've been a good boy, clean of anything hard since the Ashlee Simpson Incident."

Elyse laughed at the reference of one of my ridiculous past experiences, "Holy shit! Do you still own that shirt?"

"Yeah," I nodded, "it's gotten old, so I don't wear it regularly, but it's my trophy slash reminder to keep on keepin' on."

"It's just crazy that that ever happened," Elyse said before catching her breath and hitting the hookah. As she exhaled, the dim lighting of the lounge connected with the smoke in a way that seemed to create the illusion of distance as it outlined an attractive silhouette.

"So, you seeing anybody in New York?" I asked as casually as I could fake.

"Nah," Elyse replied, "been on a couple of dates that didn't go anywhere. Don't have the kind of time to invest in something that doesn't happen naturally." The way that I interpreted her body language led me to believe she wasn't just sparing my feelings. On the other hand, I couldn't tell whether or not the occasional jolts she had were derived from nonverbal communication or the impact of the high dose of caffeine. Either way, she was funny to watch. "How about you? Got a lady friend these days?"

"Nope. I've been on a few first dates that didn't extend to a second. I honestly haven't been out a lot. Haven't met many new people, and to go wading through my exes sounds as appealing as killing myself."

"I'm an ex, and you're here with me," Elyse shot back.

"On that note, I'm thinkin' about killing myself!" I laughed.

"Fuck you!" Elyse smiled through my cynical sarcasm.

"You are the exception. We were friends first, I understood why our relationship came to an end, and this isn't a date," I explained.

"Says you," Elyse glared at me.

Olfactory senses worked through the smoke as I finally recognized the smell of her hair. We chatted through the Turkish coffee and the tea and late into the night.

"It's been wonderful seeing you and catching up," I said as Elyse's body language suggested her desire to leave. "Honestly, getting away from the hotel and spending some time with you, this is the most normal I've felt in some time."

"When were you ever normal?" she laughed as she stirred in her seat.

"Touché," I replied.

"You ready to go?" Elyse asked to indicate that she was in fact prepared to bail.

"Yeah, I'm ready," I confirmed as I stood up to leave.

"So, you actually live at the hotel now, huh?"

"Yeah. Not exactly the place I'd want to call home, but it'll do for the time being, I guess."

"Mind if I follow you there? Maybe spend the night with ya?" Elyse offered.

"I've only got one bed," I informed

her.

Elyse rolled her eyes at me, "Well, it sounds like it's gonna work out the way I had planned."

At the end of the evening, Alem gave us everything for free minus the Turkish coffee that Elyse had already paid for. On the way out, I left what would've been the price for the hookah and tea that followed as a tip in a Blue Moon room key envelope. It was an orange envelope the size of a business card, and I had penned the name 'Alem' on it. His gracious concession deserved my appreciation, and I didn't know the next time I'd be able to show it.

10

It's been almost ten years since the Ashlee Simpson Incident.

It was the day after my last day of high school. Being my senior year, I was ready to cut loose and have a good time. I wanted to embrace my new freedom in a way that was a truly drug induced wildness.

I had arrived at the hippie festival in the early afternoon. My friend Rob and I had hitched a ride with our friend Jennifer, and the three of us had planned to meet up with some others and camp with them. We hadn't walked away from the car before some random guy gave Jennifer a prescription painkiller.

We wandered through the bloodline traffic system that consisted of tie dye for a solid half hour in the hot sun before we ran into anyone we knew.

Luckily, Rob spotted Daisy, another

girl we knew from high school, out of the crowd, and she took us to a camping area where more of our friends had set up for the weekend.

I immediately took notice of Otis eating mushrooms and asked where he'd gotten them from. He told me to be patient and explained the situation to me, "Goes like this at festivals, man, drug dealers walk proudly through the bloodline. As they pass pedestrians, they blatantly name off whatever drugs they've got for sale: rolls, mushrooms, acid, blow, whatever the fuck you're looking for. If you're interested in his products, you acknowledge his existence, otherwise he'll walk on by as though you never existed. At this point, the deal is either made or broken. You know, not everyone is smart enough to know what they're looking for- shit weed, for example."

So Otis was right; it wasn't fifteen minutes before someone walked by and muttered, "Shrooms,"

"Yes, sir," I said as I gestured with my hand and aimed for eye contact.

I ended up buying half an ounce of mushrooms, separated into two quarters. Hundred bucks, no biggie. I wrapped up one of the quarter bags, pocketed it, and started eating caps out of the other.

Not long after that, Otis gets a phone call; turns out to be Rob's mom. She had set up a camp elsewhere and wanted us all to pay her a visit. Otis, Rob, Jennifer, and I made our way to the other side of the campground and met up with Rob's mom, Rachel.

Also turned out Rachel had the best sheet acid at the whole festival. No joke. I bought a ten strip, ate four on the spot, and stored the rest away as the mushrooms were just starting to take effect. It was such a good day to this point.

Next thing I know, we're at the stage. The Wailers were performing without Bob Marley because, you know, he's dead and all. Regardless, for music that I've always associated with calm and relaxing sensations, their live show was a polar opposite display of power and energy. It was in this moment that I had developed a new appreciation for reggae.

Next thing I know, I'm sitting in a lawn chair at Otis' camp. I'm watching the grass grow and shrink and move with the consistency of waves. While observing the ground in this impossible display, my nervous system became depressed. I'm practically bent over in my chair when Rob asked, "You do too many drugs, man?"

Looking up at him I answered, "Yeah, man. I did too many drugs."

That's when it hit me; I'm gonna die.

Of course, I wasn't aware that the hallucinogenic intake alone couldn't kill me, nor was there any convincing me otherwise as I leapt from my lawn chair and ran fifteen yards in no specific direction. At the end of my run, I lost my balance and crashed into the ground. My peripheral vision was turning white as I became the embodiment of total desperate fear.

Convinced I was faking it, Rob told me to get up. Once his dumb ass realized that I was having a problem, he helped me to my feet. The company that Otis kept didn't care too much for my episode, and wanted me to leave. Sorry for ruining your good time, guys.

Rob suggested something that helped for a moment. He explained that with his mother being a hippie, she had seen this plenty of times, that I would be safe, and everything would be fine.

I immediately associated Rachel with safety.

Rob and Jennifer escorted me through the bloodline traffic system and back to Rachel's tent.

Our arrival didn't ease my mental spinning. I was already as good as lost.

It's all a blur until I realize that I'm on my knees in Rachel's tent. Jennifer is holding my hand and telling me everything's going to be fine.

I made eye contact with Jennifer and stuck my tongue in her mouth. This was probably some last ditch sexual urge to pass on my genetics before death takes me, which will surely be at any moment!

With Rob being two and a half times the size of me, I was single-handedly grabbed by the shoulder and thrown to the ground.

They actually let me up and close to Jennifer again. This time, instead of sexually assaulting the girl, I literally grabbed her and bit her on the throat.

That's right, I BIT HER ON THE THROAT.

I know what you're thinking, but I

wasn't stable.

And no, I didn't break the skin. She was alright.

They later told me that I was the closest thing to a real zombie they'd ever seen.

So, Rob threw me violently again, and at this point, my friends were faced with a real dilemma.

"He's getting belligerent."

"He's getting violent."

"Got any duct tape? We can tape him up and let him shake it off in an extra tent we have set up."

"No, man, nobody brought any tape."

...

...

"Let's ditch him."

What wonderful friends I had.

Rob's little brother Ronny was the only one with the balls to go through with it. He led me away from their camp; all the while I was unaware of his intentions. I simply followed him as I rambled on about being dead and other such nonsense.

Ron had taken me out to the bloodline traffic. We were out by the vendor tables where people were selling pipes, hemp jewelry, pizza, grilled cheese, and whatever else appealed to these drug nuts.

Next thing I knew, Ronny was gone. I was alone. That's when I knew that I was going to die.

I could hear my heart pounding in my left ear. In my right ear I could hear the beeping pace as though I were hooked up to a heart monitor. I could also feel my heart beating in my chest. All three of these sensations were pulsating in unison. The sound in my ears and the feeling in my chest sped faster and faster until I felt my heart stop in my chest. I could no longer hear anything in my left ear until the flat line defined in the right had panned its way to the center. As this happened, a shooting pain went from my chest to my left calf, my vision turned white, I pissed myself, and fell to the ground.

At this point, I was pretty sure that I was dead.

So, when I stood up twenty seconds later, I was convinced that this was some sort of afterlife.

I was tripping harder than I care to remember, harder than I ever had in my life. My mind and body became separate entities for a period of time.

My mind went through the exhausting task of accepting the fact that I had passed. There were many points of reflection over my life as I slowly abandoned all hope of going back.

But it's not important what went on in my head; allow me to skip that part. What truly matters is what my body did during this separation.

Since the whole dying thing took place on the vendor street, it would only make sense that it started there.

FOR THE RECORD: I don't remember much of what I did after the point of dying. The following is a blurred version of what happened according to a multitude of those who claim to have witnessed it. For the best account of what took place, I've filtered several stories and will present to you that which is most consistent. It's not until I 'woke up' that I remember what was going on. I'll fill you in.

So, I'm near the vendors. I walked up to a table where pipes were being sold. I walked up to the counter, picked up a water bong, smiled at the lady behind the counter, and took off running. Yeah, first stroll through the afterlife and I'm trying to steal material possessions.

This hippie lady who knew me stops me out of the crowd and takes the bong away.

"Fuck that!" I started swearing at her. "It's my bong, damn it!"

She reeled back and slapped me hard in the face as though it would bring me out of it like it does in the movies. She hit me in the fucking face!

I growled at her and ran off into the crowd.

I got naked somewhere along the way. I threw out my favorite pair of shorts which held two hundred in cash, my ID, all of the drugs I didn't do, and my pride. I also threw away my favorite Pink Floyd t-shirt, my underwear, and my glasses. Yeah, my fucking glasses. By the way, I'm blind without them. You're blurry from here.

The only possessions I didn't outright throw away were my piercings and my left sock.

I got arrested. Not sure how. Over time, I've accumulated several different versions spanning from "you went peacefully" to "you were tackled/clothes lined by a huge black security guard three times your size." The truth to that event has been lost in time. Doesn't matter; I got arrested.

When I finally 'woke up,' I was alone in a dimly lit space, strapped down to a table.

Now, I was convinced that this was some distant layer of hell where I was to be subjected to scientists who wanted to slice me open and play with my insides. The whole mess was rather frightening and more so while I was under the impression that I deserved it. The straps were tight, and my movement was restricted.

My first plan of escape was to close my eyes. I figured I'd open them elsewhere, considering this had been the ongoing fashion since I had died. I dreamed a vivid drug induced sequence of sunshine and horror.

When I opened my eyes again, I came to witness the real horror that was the same place I had been. I pissed on myself in disappointment. Couldn't see very well either. With such blurred vision, it was difficult to study my surroundings.

I was strapped down in the far left corner of this space. There was a light around the corner of the other end of the room. I was alone and wearing an Ashlee Simpson t-shirt; pre nose job. My left sock was the only other article of clothing that I had on at that point. I quickly realized that the ground was made out of grass and that the wall ended at the ground. I was in a tent!

Sounds of hippie music and fireworks made their way to my ears from the distance, and that's when it hit me; not only was I not dead, I was still at the festival!

I had to get out of there!

I began picking at the straps. I got my right arm completely free and started picking at the left when a uniformed police officer walked in on me.

"What the fuck are you doing?" he shouted at me. Three other officers followed him in, and they strapped me down again.

One of them threw a towel over my dick as he said, "Cover yourself, boy!" Then they left.

Wonderful. Shit. I was pretty sure I'd rather be dead than in this situation.

I was able to gyrate the towel off of me and to the ground. Who needs modesty at a time like this?

I also started picking at the straps again. They were tighter this time around. No problem; the illusion of privacy also affords patience.

I was halfway through the first strap when they walked in again. Outraged by my attempt to get out, they again tightened the straps.

"You see this, boy?" the angry pig yelled. He held something in his hand and shook it at me.

Like I said earlier, "you're blurry from here," so I said, "No. I can't see anything."

It didn't matter that I couldn't see it, he proceeded to threaten me with it anyway, "If you try to get out again, I'm gonna break your fuckin' fingers!"

Terrified, the only thought running through my head as the police left was, "I've gotta do this shit faster," as I went back to work on the straps.

The police officer returned, and I played it off as though I were cool. He left, and I went back to work. Yeah, that's right. I'm smooth.

Pig man came back.

I tried to play it off again.

"What are you doing?"

Busted; I looked up at him and angrily cried out, "Fuck you!"

"Fuck you!" he yelled back.

We started swearing back and forth. You may think of this as a bad situation, but this was in fact a good thing for our relationship. We were establishing communication. A few more words were exchanged before the officer realized that the kid strapped down to the table wasn't completely insane anymore.

That's when he said, "Hey, man, I'm going to undo one of your straps, and since you're so good at it, you can undo the other. Then we're gonna talk."

I became excited, "Yeah, yeah, talk. Good. Let's talk."

He undid the strap and freed my left arm.

The feeling of being free and knowing they weren't going to strap me down again had caused this shift in momentum as I rolled off of the table and fell to the floor. I rose to my knees and untied the strap that had restrained my right arm. Standing up, I pulled down Ms. Simpson to cover my genitals as I approached the officer.

With his arms crossed and a stern look on his face he plainly said, "You can't run around naked. Not even at Hippie Fest."

I looked up at him and boldly inquired, "Where are my pants?"

To which he replied, "You didn't come in with any."

I thought for a moment before asking, "Do you have some pants somewhere? This is a big event. They've gotta have a necessities tent. A trash bag? Anything I can use to cover my junk so that I can walk around in public!"

"No, man, we don't have anything for you."

I thought for a moment and considered my options before asking, "What if I don't have any pants?"

"We're gonna have to take you to jail."

I don't know about you, but I've never heard any good stories from anyone who has been to jail. So, I panicked and actually looked around the tent for pants.

Through distorted vision, I found a dark blur in the grass.

Yep.

Five feet to the left of the table to which I had been strapped down, in the grass was a discarded pair of sexy black lace panties. In disgust, I swallowed the last of the pride that I pretended to have as I picked them up and asked, "If I put these on, will you let me go?"

The officer's serious face broke away

to a smile as he said, "Yeah, man, you put those on, and I will let you go."

So, I put on the panties.

He got a laugh out of it, showed me off to a few of his pig buddies, and complained that nobody had had a camera on hand. He then released me into the night.

The last time I remember anything the sun was high in the sky, and now it's the middle of the night. I can recognize vendor art from earlier, but I had lost all sense of direction when it came to the topic of my friends and their camps.

So, I wandered in my genetic blindness. Wearing the Ashlee Simpson shirt and the panties, I bluntly asked strangers for help. Even though you're blurry from here, I can still make out that your facial expression is saying, "What the fuck is wrong with that guy?"

I wandered around like this for half an hour or so before some random person came up behind me, grabbed my shoulder, and said, "Come with me, man, we've gotta get you some pants before they arrest you again."

I never caught the guy's name, but he was my personal savior that night. He took me to his camp and actually gave me a pair of swishy gym pants. The stranger then asked if there was anything else he could do to help. I asked him if he had a working cell phone on hand. He did, and he let me use it.

I called Otis as his number was the only one I had bothered to memorize and arranged to meet up with him at a pizza shack on the vendor street.

None of the guys thought that I was sane. Those losers sent Rachel to save my ass. She took me back to camp where they fed me two oversized pot brownies. I was still tripping visually, but I was stable and peacefully coming down.

That was the end of my first day at the festival. It would later be the event known as the 'Ashlee Simpson Incident' as it redefined my reputation for many of the years that followed.

11

Working the desk the following morning was dreadful as I had gotten minimal sleep. To have had Elyse stay the night was well worth the price of being tired the next day. Letting her sleep in as I went down to work the desk, she was awake and in the lobby by half past nine offering to pick up something for me to eat before heading home. What a doll!

Wolfgang caught a glimpse of her and approached me about it after she had gone. With an ear to ear smile spread across his face, he called me out, "I see you have old girlfriend with you last night, eh! I see Elyse leave this morning. That's good, man. She still look super hot, number one! How you get her here?"

"Thanks," I laughed. "She's in town until the New Year and wanted to see me. I was surprised, too." Thanks to Wolfgang's prying eyes, the entire staff would soon know that I had gotten laid.

"I thought you had written off that ho!" Otis laughed in revealing that the news had made it to him before he had even arrived for his shift the following Monday.

"Shit. Do we have to go over this?" I asked.

"My little man's all growed up!" Otis choked out.

"It's not meant to last, and I'm not pretending it is, man. I know what I'm getting myself into," I lied through my teeth.

"So, you're not in denial about her plans to bail on you again?" Otis was blunt.

"We're not the type to do the long distance thing, and she's heading home after the holidays. Don't bust my chops, man."

"I'm just looking out for you, sir. Don't need a repeat of a couple years back. Hey, Jessie, at least she's real this time! I'm just glad you're not getting hand jobs from Cheryl anymore," Otis laughed.

"Hand jobs from Cheryl? She may do that shit with some of the guests or Wolfgang, but you're crazy to think I'd ever go for that," I said as I attempted to hold my ground. "We all know you occasionally help a prostitute to their room and 'hang out' with them for fifteen minutes or so."

Otis' eyes focused on me as he came back with, "I was just trying to convince her that you usually cry after fuckin' em."

"Fuck you," I laughed.

"So, what's up today? Any crazies?" Otis asked for the daily news.

"Not really. Oh, but speaking of

prostitutes, we received some promotional soap from some human trafficking group earlier today," I said.

"Human trafficking soap? You seem pretty excited," Otis observed in his skepticism.

"Check it out!" I said as I walked towards the time clock where I had left the package. "It came with this folder with prostitution statistics from Crawford County, Indiana."

"Wrong state if they're trying to hit home," Otis pointed out.

"Yeah, but they've got their hearts in the right place. From a corporate standpoint, it's wasteful. We can't give these out to people!" I said as I opened a shoe box that contained hundreds of individually wrapped travel sized bars of soap. I lifted one out and handed it to Otis for him to read the sticker on the back of each bar.

"'Are you being forced to do anything you do not want to do? Have you been threatened if you try to leave? Have you witnessed young girls being prostituted? If so, please call: National Human Trafficking Hotline.' Holy shit. This for real?" Otis asked, dumbfounded.

"Yeah, man," I replied.

"What do we do with 'em? Give 'em out at our discretion? That's just begging for problems. I don't want to hand these out."

"I'm in the same boat," I said, "they're a great gesture. I even thought about just using this box in all of the rooms until it's gone but,"

"But that's a fucking stupid idea in

terms of business. Pretty much waves the flag that says, 'Hey, we're admitting prostitution happens here regularly!'"

"First off, I understand that, but anyone who comes to a low-end place like this should know that rampant prostitution and drug use takes place where they intend to rest their heads. Secondly, Martinez told me the same thing, that it was a fucking stupid idea."

"You called Martinez over hooker soap?" Otis was so surprised that he showed difficulty in handling the information.

"I knew it was a long shot. I don't really want to deal with it either, but it seemed to be a rather intuitive way to address the situation instead of ignoring it as we typically do," I argued.

"You actually intended to hand this shit out," Otis said shaking the bar that he was still holding, "at our discretion or blanket them in every room? You really considered that an option? Adam was right; you are fucking stupid."

"What else are we gonna do with 'em?" I put my hands in the air.

I ended up taking the entire shoe box of about three to four hundred bars up to my apartment for personal use.

There was an event that left me feeling troubled. While working a desk shift, I received a call from room 319. The guest had already vacated, and I was being called by the housekeeper assigned to clean it. She wanted to inform me that a lot of drugs and paraphernalia had been left and asked if I'd want to take a look or do something about it.

Putting up the sign to inform guests that I was away and would be back momentarily, I went up to the room to find a wonderland of hard drug partying. In the bathroom I found ashes and blood stained washcloths in the sink and bathtub. On the backside of the toilet tank I found what appeared to be a makeup bag that contained two dirty needles. In the actual sleeping space I found a tin foil crack pipe on the floor next to the bed that was furthest from the window. The work desk was layered in ash and had pills scattered on it that I recognized as Vicodin from my days of drug abuse.

"Think this is enough to be worth calling the cops?" the housekeeper asked me after I had witnessed the wreckage.

"Yeah, I think I'll give 'em a call for sure," I answered.

The end result was that the police never came. I actually received a phone call from the police station about two hours after I had called them to inform me that it was simply a busy day, that my call was important, and that someone would be out as soon as possible. No one showed up except for the dirt bag druggie who had the room registered to his name and wanted to rent it again for another night. I told the addict to "fuck himself" and turned him away. I held up my end of the job while the police must've had better things to do than care about the happenings at a dump like the Blue Moon Inn.

A week into December and business

was dead. The slowing down of business was expected as the time between the last OSU home football game and the Arnold Fitness Classic in March made the Blue Moon a relative ghost town. The staff had accepted Adam's departure and had adjusted to the change by slacking off even more so than before, something I didn't think was possible. We were lucky to sell thirty rooms a night, which was nothing compared to the typical seventy to ninety during the warmer months. The chill of the approaching winter layered everything in a frost that consumed the landscape from dusk to dawn, and our staff was torn over it. The front desk loved the winter months as it enabled the inner sloth, while the housekeeping department dreaded it as less rooms sold equated to the cutting of hours.

I had found a way to avoid being on the desk as often as I had been. While Abdul wanted nothing to do with the extra morning shifts, Anna was willing to cross train in order to preserve some of her hours during the winter. She worked with Otis and me for the first week of December, and from there she was good to run it on her own.

Being free from the desk resulted in working from my apartment for the majority of the things I could accomplish from there. Sorting through audit reports, placing orders for what we needed to keep the hotel running, and paying the bills became something I fumbled through as I was doing it all myself for the first time. Adam typically did the tedious stuff while I used to offer my hand to the housekeepers or Wolfgang, hanging around to make sure the place didn't burn down as I had often wished it would.

Today was Anna's first shift on the desk by herself. When I finally went down to the lobby area to prepare the bank run, Wolfgang was standing at the desk, presumably hitting on Anna while she looked bored.

"Good morning, Mr. President! How you this morning?" Wolfgang announced my arrival in a loud and booming voice as he typically did.

"I'm alright. How are you two doing?" I asked.

"Mr. President?" Anna laughed.

I shook my head and smiled, "He's been calling me that for years."

"Well, when I first come to America it was Clinton, then Bush, and now Obama. But I think Jessie be best president of all someday."

"You thought Bush was a good president?" Anna asked in a smug tone.

Wolfgang shrugged, "Yeah. He no Jesus. How he worse than Obama or Clinton?"

Anna's liberal bias really threw her for a loop, "You're kidding me, right?"

"Listen, lady," Wolfgang started, "before I come to America, I spend lot of time in Germany. Germany beautiful too! Someday I hope to go back and live there again. Before Germany, I grow up in Czechoslovakia, spend lot of time in Bosnia. I grow up with piece of shit people killing each other over nothing! I come to America and the people have political differences, a divide so great that families argue and fight when they meet over holidays. I no expert on American politics, but no matter how much you no like President Bush or I no care for President Obama, I never once see people bombing or killing each other in street. I know it happen here sometime, but not like mein home country. Not even close."

Anna nodded to express that she understood as she said, "Bush was still pretty bad."

"I no see economy getting much better." Wolfgang shot back.

Preparing the bank statement in the back office, I asked how Anna felt about being alone on the desk. She claimed that she felt bored, but she seemed to be finding ways to keep herself entertained between her smart phone and the full access front desk computers that allowed for aimless surfing online. It literally only blocked out pornography and video games, leaving much to do and find for those looking to whittle away at their respective shift.

As I hopped into my car for the bank run, I started the engine and sat back as I turned on the CD player. *Kind of Blue* by Miles Davis sprang to life, and I let the opening track play through as the car warmed up. The damn thing was about fifteen hundred miles overdue for an oil change, but I would put it off a bit longer with the hopes that another mild day would roll through.

While waiting for the car to warm up, Wolfgang emerged from the stairwell at the far end of the building. His eyes darted back and forth before he came to the conclusion that the coast was clear. He then jumped into Wesley Johnson's 2011 Volvo and left for what I assumed was a lunch break where he'd meet up with his sugar momma or some other girl he had on the side. He may have been a scumbag who cheated on his wife and lived by a hypocritical double standard, but while the housekeepers would express disgust amongst themselves, Otis and I couldn't help but to laugh at how ridiculous it all seemed. Otis and I honestly figured that someday his wife, or his sugar momma, or just one of his side girlfriends would show and straight up murder him. Strange how in the four years I've worked with Wolfgang that we've never had any of his ladies show up to make a scene. It seemed to be a time bomb that was long overdue, and yet all we could do was wait.

12

Sleep has become difficult. It used to be so easy once I hit my twenties. I had been a restless teenager who slept very little and had convinced myself that I suffered from some sleeping disorder, but as I got older, I came to find that I was tired most of the time. The struggle to get to sleep and stay down for the night seemed to vanish as I balanced a work and school routine that demanded the majority of what I had to offer. Since then I've come to know exhaustion as most nights I turn off the light and am out with it.

Problems have returned when it comes to sleep, but once again I know it's more or less based on mental conditioning. The exhaustion is still there, but the moment I close my eyes I see those two severed fingers with the bright orange nail polish offering a peace sign on my doorstep. I see the girl I found in 113. I've become clingy with paranoia as the hotel beneath my room is a hive of constant activity; every noise that penetrates through the darkness from below leads me to check the doorstep to see if any new tidings of human remains have been left. The only night I didn't see the bright orange tips of Penelope's cold fingers was the night Elyse had stayed with me.

I had taken a step away from email and actually called Elyse a week after our Third World outing to see if she'd be interested in getting together again. She didn't answer, and when she hadn't responded three days later I figured I'd just leave her alone. Assuming I had been used for a one night stand was alright with me as I had zero expectations for the whole ordeal. There was no denying that I cared, but I had been down that road before. Once they stop calling you back, it's best to consider it the end of the affair and move forward, lest you upgrade to stalker status.

The second week in December was coming to a close when Elyse returned my call. She apologized for having not gotten back to me sooner and requested we spend another evening together, dinner and a movie kind of deal. I obliged and suggested whatever new zombie flick was out at the time as Elyse and I have had many good times making fun of those kinds of films. Knowing it would be terrible and follow the faddy trends that all zombie movies had suffered in the past decade and a half, Elyse was all for it as she recommended Sunday evening.

Thinking of myself as foolish, I knew I still loved her. I could admit it to myself, and now I had been enabled to build back up to the inevitable letdown. No matter how bad it hurts in the end, if I can just enjoy the moment, then this life will not have been wasted.

Other than the bank run, I took that Sunday off of work. Anna was holding down the desk that morning, and all of the housekeepers had shown up. Samantha would be taking over to run the second shift that day. With nothing to worry about, I figured I'd get a phone call if the place caught fire or something terrible happened as I intended to not return to the hotel until after the movie.

Once I had completed the bank run, I went to a coffee shop nearby and ordered a black coffee with an onion bagel that I had lightly buttered. I also purchased a newspaper and read in the corner for a couple of hours in order to kill time without going home.

Reading about the typical mess between Israel and Palestine, I came to find that I was apathetic to their conflict. It's such a complicated issue, but I had carried my own theories about solutions. I once cared about peace in the Middle East. It was irrelevant noise that I had exploited to occupy my time. Local crime and corruption lined the community section in a way that seemed normal. I read on to see that the Buckeyes were set to start the next season sitting pretty in the rankings and thought of how sad it was that the only good news I could seem to find was related to the football team for whom I cheered.

"I don't want you to feel like you're being used." Elyse was up front about her motives. "I had a wonderful night the last time we got together, and I really do enjoy your company."

"I understand. And no, I don't feel used. If anything, we're using each other. I'm happy with this evening alone." I shrugged, "Doesn't bother me to share a moment with you. I'd rather think of it that way- sharing moments with each other."

Elyse nodded as she took a sip from her wine glass. We had decided on an Italian place that's in between the hotel and the movie theater, "In that case, you wouldn't mind me staying with you tonight?"

The restaurant was literally three buildings down from the Blue Moon, and I'd never actually eaten there. Elyse ordered some strange layered dish that I couldn't pronounce while I went with boring and ordered chicken Alfredo, a personal favorite that's usually pretty safe when trying a new Italian restaurant. It wasn't the best, but it was damn good for a chain.

The zombie movie was fun. I think the best part about the whole thing was putting my arm around Elyse and having her there. Plus, it had my favorite classic ending; everybody dies!

"Rape scenes are just weird to watch," Elyse pointed out in the theater parking lot as we left, "especially with other people. I think the worst was watching the Swedish version of *Girl with the Dragon Tattoo* with my parents. Salander gets that first punch right in the face, and it's just downhill from there. Seeing her fight against the current with my dad sitting next to me was about as awkward as it gets."

"Agreed. No matter what movie it is, rape scene comes along, all I can do to get through it is eat candy," I admitted.

"Holy shit," Elyse said as her eyes widened, "you opened your malted milk balls when the sexual assault started! I didn't think anything of it at the time. You're sick, Jessie." She laughed through the realization. "This must be a recent development because I remember watching films with rape scenes in them with you, and you never did any ritualistic thing back then."

"As you said, recent development. Those past experiences were traumatizing. I've just found a way to mentally protect myself," I said as we got into my car.

"You don't have to lie to me. You do it for shits 'n giggles, huh?"

"Yeah," I admitted, "when I'm watching a movie with friends and it pops up, they almost expect it now. It's a way to cut through the tension of watching a rape scene and keeps the mood light."

"Doesn't that go against the feeling that the movie is trying to convey?"

"Yeah, but I'm scum of the earth. There's something about consuming sugar while witnessing the fictitious suffering of others that I find pretty soothing."

"Fictitious or not, you're sick as shit," Elyse said. She was pretty used to me and didn't appear to actually be shocked or disgusted by what I had said.

We returned to the hotel to find Samantha reading some romance novel in the back office. "Slow night?" I asked as we walked in.

"Yeah," Samantha said without taking her eyes away from the book.

Sunday nights were typically slow, so I asked no further questions. If Samantha didn't have anything she wanted to tell me, then operations must be going smoothly.

Elyse and I went up to my apartment via the stairwell. She suggested we take the elevator, and I told her that unless I was hauling something that I couldn't manage on the stairs, a housekeeping cart for example, I always went up on foot.

Once we got to the private concrete stairwell that separated the third floor from my apartment, I became somewhat concerned that we'd find more fingers or something of the sort since I had been out all day. Luckily, the doorstep was clear and my paranoia seemed unjustified.

Then we went inside. I opened the door, and Elyse went into the darkness first. I followed her in and took no notice until she pointed it out, "I see you've rearranged your apartment since the last time I was here."

Turning on the lights to see that my living room had been rearranged, I spared Elyse the fear that was taking hold of my nerves as I said, "Yeah, moved some stuff around. Felt like the place needed a shakeup." The couch and television had been rearranged to face the opposite direction as they previously had. The desktop computer and the entire system that accompanied it had been moved across the room next to the sliding glass door. I went to my bedroom to see that my bed had also been relocated from the center of the room to the far corner. My eyes scanned both for my belongings to see if anything had been stolen and for anything left behind like a note or something. The Sauer pistol was missing from the bread drawer. The entity had stolen my gun! To the best of my ability to search without giving away that something was wrong, I took notice that an artificial Christmas tree that was only about three feet tall had been decorated with lights that the intruder had placed in my garden and left on for me to find. I calmed down as best I could and tried to enjoy Elyse's company, while in the back of my mind I was panicking over the thought that some entity had played Manson Family and moved everything around in my apartment. Had they possibly set up some kind of recording device? Racing thoughts distracted me from the beautiful woman who was there to spend time with me, and the moment we shared was awkwardly complicated. At least I was able to play it off as to not burden her with my worries.

We had breakfast at midnight as I scrambled some eggs, fried some bacon, and toasted a couple pieces of wheat bread. Considering the hour, we drank high pulp orange juice instead of coffee, as Elyse was looking to get some sleep that night.

After Elyse had fallen asleep, I got out of bed and did a more thorough search of the apartment. Stepping out onto the cold roof with bare feet, I inspected the tree; it's decorative lights were the only thing enabling my inspection in the night as the parking lot lights were too far off and obstructed by the building to pollute this patio area. The bitter cold stung my feet until they went numb. I then unplugged the tree's lights and went back inside. Once I had come to the conclusion that no recording devices were left for my surveillance, I gently crawled back into bed next to Elyse. The shock of the intrusion prevented me from sleeping that night, though I must admit it was nice to listen to the rhythm of her breathing.

13

Paranoia crept over me as the daylight dwindled in the approaching winter. Two days after the Manson Family style creepy crawl that had rearranged my apartment and I still hadn't slept. With craters under my eyes and my hair unkempt, my appearance could be confused with your typical junkie around here. I had withdrawn and had all but stopped communicating with the staff beyond what was absolutely necessary. Not wanting to let the staff think I was weak or something bad was happening, I explained that I had been feeling under the weather and was taking most of the paperwork to my apartment as to not spread my germs around. The option to work alone became my excuse to literally isolate myself.

Elyse had gone home the following morning after catching the same breakfast we had shared the previous evening, except that we had opted to brew coffee instead of having juice.

Wanting to leave the impression or create the illusion that I was not leaving the property to run the daily deposits to the bank, I started using Wesley Johnson's Volvo while leaving my Oldsmobile parked in plain view near the main office entrance. It was such a smooth ride that I had wished it didn't belong to a dead man. With the veil of paranoia clouding my judgment, I felt that I deserved to take it for a spin every now and again.

It was that second day after my date with Elyse that this whole mess got all the more complicated. Having not slept, I dropped into the lobby to open the safe and prepare the deposit. Anna was preoccupied with her smart phone and the occasional guest to care to make anything further than small talk, which was fine by me.

The chill of the weather had urged me to move on from hooded sweatshirts to finally breaking out my leather jacket for the first time that season. After preparing the bank deposit, I grabbed Wesley's keys and went back to the stairwell. From there, I went up to the second floor, took a right down that hallway and went to the stairwell at the far end of the building, descended, and emerged at the far end of the building near the dumpsters where Wolfgang and I had left the Volvo.

Concealed in the shade of the building, a layer of frost was built upon the windows of the vehicle. Opening the door, I

started the car without climbing in so that I
could scrape the windows while it warmed
up. I peered into the backseat to look for an
ice scraper. I found nothing and hoped that
one would be in the trunk so that I wouldn't
have to get mine out of my car. There was a
'pop trunk' button on the inside of the driver
side door that I lightly pressed. I heard a
sudden pop as I watched the trunk lift up
automatically.

Hoping the clutter would be minimal
so that I could quickly find the ice scraper, I
was horrified as I took the few steps around
the car to find a dead girl in the middle of
the oversized trunk. She was curled into a
fetal position, and her facial expression
looked to be of a peaceful daze. Frost had
accumulated on her eyelashes. Wearing
short shorts and a tank top, it was pretty
obvious to me that she was a junkie as her
cold limbs were lined with track marks.
There were no signs of violence, if you didn't
count what she had done to herself, so who
was trying to hide this girl? Even with the
chill of the air, there was still some color to
her face which forced me to conclude that
she hadn't been dead for very long. I felt like
crying for this waste of life before me, but all
I could bring myself to do was bite my lip
and sigh heavily as the weight of it piled on
top of this burden.

Closing the trunk, I decided it would
be best to take my car on the bank run.
Turning off Wesley's car, I went back into
the building through the stairwell at the end
and maneuvered my way back to the main
lobby where I returned the keys to the

Volvo.

The problem could no longer be ignored as time seemingly continued to move forward without me. I had been back from the bank and was barricaded in my apartment when Anna called me at two o'clock that afternoon.

"Hello," I meekly answered the phone. I suddenly felt dizzy and sick to my stomach as I wanted nothing to do with this phone call. If I could only neglect my responsibilities and ignore the world away, I may find some sort of relief. There would be no such luck as the weight of the storm had collapsed and was crashing down upon my head.

"Jessie, it's Anna. I need you to come to the lobby."

"What's going on?" I asked plainly.

"Estela found three people dead in room 136. Looks like drugs, but I'm not sure."

"Fuck," was all I could bring myself to say before hanging up on Anna. Our conversation didn't need to go any further, and I simply hung up on her. In the desolate silence that was the isolation of my apartment, I started to weep as I repeated the only word that made any sense in that moment, "Fuck."

Wanting to see the damage first hand before moving forward, I made a key to room 136 and went straight there instead of the lobby. Anna was right as I found two boys and one girl on the twin beds. One couple held each other while the second boy had his arms draped across the bed as though he had been holding someone. A set of needles were placed on the nightstand between the two beds and appeared stained with the filth of some hard drug. They looked to be about the same age as the girl in the trunk, which made me think they had all come together and someone had failed in moving the bodies in order to hide it. Their expressions were hauntingly pleasant as they all seemed to be sleeping.

I just stood there for a moment in between the twin singles and watched over them, hoping that they'd wake up from my nightmare, ask what the hell I was doing in their hotel room, and life would go on. I even fantasized about it before realizing I could taste the salt of my own tears.

Hoping that the police would actually come this time, I went to the office to make the call and report Estela's findings. In order to keep my hands as clean as possible, I neglected to tell them about finding the girl in the trunk of the Volvo. Hopefully, a certain someone will come and clean up the mess before an investigation leads them to the car with my finger prints on it.

While waiting for the police, I scanned over the Onity key reports to see that they were issued two keys when they checked in with Samantha the previous day and that no duplicates were made until the one I had just programmed. From there, I took another key tool from Onity; a black box the size of an original Game Boy was used to program and read card use on individual locks throughout the property. Returning to 136 with the black box, I used it to find that the door had in fact been opened at one thirty that morning by housekeeping key number two. This would've happened during Cheryl's shift.

The police were little interested in an investigation. I had even gone as far as to ask what could be done, to which I was met with the reply, "The fuck do you think this is? Foul play? It's nothing more than a case of drug addicts overdosing on this batch of killer heroin that's been going around. Fuck it. There's not much we can do, and unless you've got any further information, I don't really care."

I nodded to imply that I understood the police officer.

By the time the police had left, Otis was working the desk. He had been in long enough to catch the gist of what was going on as he said, "So, it looks like the police only show up when there's a body, huh?"

Shaking my head in disbelief I said, "Yeah, man, it looks that way."

"You alright, Jessie?" Otis asked with a genuine concern in his voice.

"Been a long day. Ever since Adam left I've been overwhelmed. Job's too much for me, I guess. Haven't been sleeping well lately. I'm just stressed out, and college aged kids dying in my hotel doesn't make the day any easier," I explained.

Otis nodded as he said, "I hear that. No matter how many drug addicts and prostitutes we run outta here, there's just no stopping 'em. I know how to get into the safe and Wolfgang used to do bank runs for Adam all the time back in the day. You should take a day or two off and sleep or something."

"Or something," I echoed.

"Well, if you're looking to wind down, Ronny has some weed," Otis suggested as he lifted his inhaler to his face.

"Wow. A joint does sound pretty good about now, but I haven't gone through Ronny in a long time. I don't even think I have his number anymore."

Otis shrugged. "I don't think Ron would mind if I passed his digits to you."

Staying in the office while Otis worked, I stuck around to intercept reporters and point them to our corporate media hotline with any inquiries they had about the incident. It felt nice to pass the buck on this situation as I didn't want to answer questions.

The only person I had to answer to was Martinez who called my cell phone directly while I was still in the office. I wanted nothing more than to wrap up the conversation as soon as it started. Flipping open the obsolete phone, I said, "Hello," in a firm tone in an attempt to hide weakness or shame.

"What the fuck is going on down there?" Martinez yelled to kick off the dialog.

"Three kids checked into room 136 yesterday and were found dead by the housekeeper assigned to clean the room. Apparent overdose. The police have been here, and we've been redirecting all inquires to the media hotline," I explained.

"Cut the shit, Jessie. Why didn't you call me immediately? Unacceptable!"

Martinez's tone got uglier with every word.

"I don't have an excuse. What else do you want?" I asked.

"I want you to do your fucking job, and file the incident report! Fucking now!" Martinez yelled.

"I'll get right on that," I dryly recited.

There was a hesitation before Martinez reacted with venom, "Listen to me, you little faggot, if I could I'd fire you right now, but I don't have another option on the table. I also don't have the kind of convenience to wait around while you're fucking off! Trust me, once Adam's replacement gets in there, you may be out of a job."

"Why don't I just walk out now?" I asked.

"There's the possibility that ice may form under your feet. Thin as it'll be, if you get the report in before the business day ends, the higher ups won't have a reason to throw you away. With that in mind, it would be difficult to terminate you without the sort of due process we'll eventually go through," Martinez explained.

"I can't wait to take you down with me," I said in a smug tone.

"Wh- What are you rambling about? You little prick..." Martinez seemed to hesitate and stumble a bit over his words.

"I actually have photographs of you taking known local prostitutes into one of our hotel rooms during a previous visit," I started.

Martinez scoffed, "My immediate boss is a personal friend of twenty years. My wife and I are estranged. You dare threaten to blackmail me? You've got nothing, you little faggot. I will make you disappear if you pursue fucking with me! You understand?"

"I also know that you've taken the maximum daily amount of petty cash from the drawers of each property under your supervision multiple times during numerous visits equating to somewhere between two and three thousand dollars in the last six months. Not sure about your immediate boss, Rick, but I've met a couple of people that are higher than him. You would threaten to make me disappear for cramping your style, but I'll promise you that I'll burn this place and your image to the ground." I fought fire with piss while Otis soaked up the entertainment as he overheard my side of the conversation.

"This chat has degraded a little too far for my tastes. Why don't we wrap this up, cool down, and talk again sometime soon once we've collected ourselves. I've been in this business long enough to tell that you can't handle your current position, but if you stick it out until Charlie gets there in three weeks, we'll live and let live," Martinez offered a compromise.

"You're right about one thing. I can't handle the job when the surrounding area falls apart and the wreckage takes refuge where I conduct business. I'm not sure how much I'll really want to keep the job after all is said and done. The truth is, I hate you Martinez. If I could, I'd harvest your fat to fuel old school lanterns," I started to ramble.

Martinez was done as he cut me off,

"Jessie, you always were a little faggot,"
which was then followed up with the click of
his slamming the phone down and hanging
up on me.

"That was awesome." Otis was in awe
as I flipped my cell phone shut.

"The context really makes all the
difference," I observed. "When Adam called
me a 'piece of shit' it was no big deal
because we were as close to friends as you
could get with a boss. When Martinez called
me a 'faggot' I just went into blackmail
mode."

"Holy shit," Otis laughed, "He called
you a fag? And what was the whole 'lanterns
from his fat' thing all about?"

Rolling my eyes as I tried to come up
with something, all that came when I spoke
was, "Heat of the moment. I was aiming for
awkward disgust."

Ronny was surprised in a good way
when I called him. He invited me over, not
only to buy some pot, but to catch up as it
had been at least a year since I'd last seen
him. All I had heard about his recent
troubles surfaced from the rumor mill,
namely Otis as he was my last connection to
that chapter of my life. I declined to go over
there that evening as I was practically
catatonic after the whole incident. Between
finding an entire group of overdosed junkies
and my boss talking down to me the way he
did, the day would be numbed with alcohol.
He understood, and we made plans for me
to drop by the next day.

Luckily, my cabinet contained half a
bottle of Bushmills Irish Whiskey that I had

leftover from my birthday. With it and a can of Coke I could hole up in my apartment for the night.

Six or seven shots into my leftovers and the apartment phone starts ringing. It was past ten o'clock, but I figured Otis needed assistance at the front desk. I lifted the receiver to my ear but didn't say anything.

A moment passed before a voice deeper than Otis' emerged from the other side, "Jessie?"

"Who is this?" I snapped.

"You sound drunk and irritated that I've got you on the phone," the voice said casually.

He was right about me being irritated, "I'm hanging up now, you bastard."

"It's Murdock. You know, Von Hertz?"

"You know how to dial to my room from yours?" I was completely bewildered at this point.

"Just admitting that I know about Penelope's fingers on your doorstep makes me suspect. Knowing that your apartment has been recently rearranged, and telling you that the three kids in that room and the one you found in the Volvo were murdered, definitely makes me suspect, but it's the only way to break the ice and offer my assistance," Von Hertz said.

Lost for words, I said the only thing that made sense- "Fuck, what all do you know?"

Von Hertz was calm and collected as he responded, "I know plenty. I'm stationed in 327 tonight. You come pay me a visit, and

I'll fill you in."

"Why not over the phone? Real quick. I don't want to see you or talk to you anymore than is absolutely necessary, but if you can point me in the right direction as to who is fucking everything up around here, you need to tell me now while you've got me on the phone!" I demanded.

"You're not in any position to tell a paranoid man to spill his secrets over a possibly tapped phone line. How drunk are you?" Murdock spoke with aggression now, "We hang up and I unplug everything in the room. From there it's up to you whether or not someone knocks on my door and talks to me like I'm worth a damn!"

"Alright man, alright! I'll be down in a moment," I slurred into the receiver.

Without another word Von Hertz hung up, leaving the ball in my court. Being drunk and having planned for isolation, the first step to leaving was putting on some pants and purging as to preserve the memory as best I could. After getting some blue jeans on, I hovered above my toilet and stuck my fingers in my throat, wasting the leftover birthday whiskey that hadn't yet left my stomach for the other organs.

Sobriety clashed with what was already in my system, and I suddenly felt close to functional again. It was then that I realized Von Hertz may somehow be behind all of this and was planning to lure me to his room so that he could get the jump on me. With the Sauer missing, I grabbed a pocket knife from my dresser drawer in case I would end up having to protect myself. Fear struck me then as I considered that if Von Hertz was behind all of this, he'd already be in possession of my gun. It just didn't make sense, though, unless he were a locksmith or computer programmer. It's relatively easy to hack into these key card readers to get into the rooms, but the stairwell and my personal door require different keys. Adam carried the only copies before he was fired.

The hallway of the third floor was dim and depressing. The yellowing paint job near the ceiling was really disgusting as I wondered if corporate would ever consider a remodel. I could just buy some new paint, team up with Wolfgang, and knock it out in a day, but I had more pressing matters at hand. As I found myself standing in front of room 327, I took a deep breath and hesitated, allowing the moment to linger on for as long as I could hold out before finally knocking on the door.

Von Hertz answered it quickly, and the door opened to a dark room; the burning of a large single candle in a glass jar on the work desk illuminated a small part of the room itself. "Come on in, Jessie." He spoke casually, "Hope you like the smell cinnamon. It's my favorite."

The dim light made it possible for me to observe my surroundings as I took notice of the line of light bulbs on top of the dresser, the refrigerator and microwave moved to the opposite corners of where they were usually stationed, the two pieces of wall art and the hanging mirrors removed from their places and set to the floor, and that every possible electronic device was unplugged for the occasion. Moments like these I wish I had upgraded to a smart phone or at least had an old school pocket-sized tape recorder. My sense of smell had been compromised from the induced vomiting, but I wouldn't acknowledge that, for me, the candle was only a source of light.

"Have a seat," Von Hertz said as he gestured to the armchair. I sat down as he did the same in the rolling work chair on the other side of the desk. "Make yourself comfortable."

"What's this all about?" I asked as we were positioned facing each other.

With a blank expression on his face Von Hertz recited, "Four one seven zero two."

Dumbfounded, there was a silence before I spoke up, "I've been wondering about that! How did you know my code for programming room keys? I've since changed it, but I've been wondering about that."

"I have my sources. We'll get to that," Von Hertz said as his twitchy eyes darted from left to right, and then panned back to me, "who else has been driving the car where you found the dead girl in the trunk?"

"Wolfgang? That Nazi wannabe is behind all of this?"

"Not exactly. That's what I've been instructed to tell you. I'm supposed to throw you off in order to buy a little more time," Von Hertz answered. "I'm at the point where I'm fearing for my life. Luckily, my photo ID is outdated in terms of my home address. On that note, I don't think I'll ever be back after tonight."

Puzzled, I tried to piece together what was going on. "Who instructed you to what? The body in the Volvo was placed there to make it look like Wolf was trying to hide the body?"

"Pretty shit job, I know. Check out my reward for lying to you," Von Hertz said as he placed a baggy that held some kind of black substance on the desk.

The light of the candle bounced off of the dirty plastic as I figured it was some sort of hard drug. "What exactly is that?"

"It's some of that death heroin that's been going around."

"Fuck," was all I could use to respond.

"You've heard about it. Traces back to a chemical factory in Mexico, kills users wholesale, literally put all four of those kids to sleep before a single one of them could react or knew what was happening. I may not be the smartest addict around, but I'm not stupid enough to get tricked into using this shit. Some fucking reward," Von Hertz explained.

"Yeah, I know about it. No more games, Murdock. Don't fuck with me on this. Who's willing to kill you to confuse me?"

"Otis," he said in a tone deeper than usual.

"Really?" I inquired.

"If you can't read between the lines by now, this conversation is over. He's been bragging to me about it for quite some time. 'Vigilante justice' he calls it. He's gone all out! I know all about the death junk Otis has been passing out, and that approach is rather tame compared to some other methods he's described."

"Such as?" I said as I put my hand up, expecting gruesome details.

"Doesn't matter. What does matter is that he has the keys to your apartment! What matters is that he's got your gun! He's been making room keys with your code for a long time now in order to make it look like you've been involved the entire time. Whether or not he decides to kill you, you're going down, Jessie. You're going fucking down." Von Hertz explained in the flickering light as I smelled the cinnamon scented candle for the first time.

14

    Following the conversation with Von Hertz, I went back to my apartment and decided that I would be going out for the night after all. I brewed a pot of coffee to continue the sobering process and caught a shower as I looked like an absolute wreck. By the time I had dried off and gotten two cups of coffee in my system, I felt as refreshed as one could after that whole mess.

    The time was well into Cheryl's shift, but I still took the side stairwell to avoid running into Otis in the likely case that Cheryl was late. I planned on committing a cardinal sin and going to the Wal-Mart. Elyse would frown upon such endeavors, but that was not the time to consider a politically motivated approach to economics. They were the only place that would be open at that time of night that would be carrying what I was looking for.

The night air was crisp, and I felt alive as it hit my face for the first time since the cold season had arrived, I felt some sort of relief. I didn't want to believe Otis had been killing people with drugs or through more violent methods, but unless Von Hertz was really out to throw me for a loop, for which he deserves an Oscar, everything but a motive was clear and made sense to me.

While driving to Wal-Mart, I called Ronny. Figuring drug dealers operated at all hours of the night, he didn't mind taking my call shortly after midnight as he confirmed that he had just started watching a movie and would probably be awake until sometime near dawn. I was relieved to hear his business plan hadn't changed very much since I had last seen him. Hoping Ronny could offer some insight to Otis' activities, I planned for him to know nothing.

Based on the hour, I was hoping that Wal-Mart would be pretty quiet. With less than a week until Christmas, the damn place was a frenzy of last minute panic that consisted of indiscriminate consumerism, weeping, and gnashing of teeth. Making my way towards the electronics department was no easy feat, but once I was there, I quickly purchased a security surveillance system with three camera units that would send a digital audio and visual feed to my computer.

After using my emergency credit card and getting out of Wal-Mart, I secured my new electronics in the trunk of my car and drove the long way to Ron's apartment complex so that I could listen to some music and give some thought to the bigger picture.

The neighborhood seemed run down and out of shape as I parked my car facing a neglected fenced-off tennis court. The tattered nets swayed in the breeze as though they were hoping to intercept someone's poor serve.

"Sup, man?" Ronny said as he answered the door to his second story apartment in a tie dye muscle shirt and a pair of dirty grey sweatpants. His hair was buzzed and much shorter than he typically liked it due to recent court appearances.

"Not too much, sir," I said as I entered his apartment and gave him a hug. "Got sidetracked from my drinking and thought I'd swing by here instead."

The place was less dirty than I had expected. It was obvious that they didn't know about the invention of the vacuum cleaner, but there was little in the way of clutter on the tables or floor. An overflowing ashtray and the dust of incense layered over the living room table, but there was space where I expected to find dishes holding the remains of half-eaten meals. Numerous pipes were scattered about on shelves, the kitchen counter, and the living room table. All in all, I counted seven glass bowls. The same Grateful Dead tapestry that Ronny has had since high school covered the entirety of the wall next to the front door, while various band posters and portraits done by friends decorated the place. There was a neglected acoustic guitar in the furthest corner of the room next to the sliding glass door that exited to their petite balcony.

"Been a little bit, Jessie," Jeremy Cross said as he emerged from the bathroom. He wore pajama pants and a white muscle shirt to show off his numerous tattoos.

Not wanting to appear put off by Cross' presence, I replied, "Yes, it has. How ya been?"

"Alright, alright. Just chillin' for the most part," he said as he sat down on the couch.

"Have a seat, man. We're just about to start the first *Lord of the Rings* movie," Ron gestured toward the television, "or you wanna get to business first?"

"Yeah, let's take care of that if you don't mind," I responded. "I still find it hard to believe that they're turning *The Hobbit* into a trilogy of its own while *The Lord of the Rings* got crushed into one movie per book."

"I think that'll make it the best in terms of attention to detail, man," Ronny said as he and I went into his bedroom while Jeremy waited on the couch.

There was a different kind of glass pipe that rested next to a dirty lamp on his nightstand that I assumed was used for smoking crystal meth, a habit I figured Ronny would've grown out of by now. The nightstand was the only piece of furniture in the room other than a mattress that sat next to it. Clothes were piled up in various locations, and clutter was more abundant here than it was in the living room.

Ron opened the door to the nightstand and removed a weighted safe where he kept his business money and supplies. After entering the numerical code on the keypad, I heard a click as the little door popped open to reveal a wad of cash and various substances wrapped in plastic.

"How much ya lookin' for, buddy?" Ron asked as he pulled out the bag that contained the pot.

"Eighth still goin' for fifty?" I answered his question with a question.

"Yes, sir."

"I think I'll go with a quarter," I nodded as I pulled my wallet from my back pocket and handed the man five twenty dollar bills.

"Can do," Ronny said cheerfully as he removed a small digital scale from the safe and weighed out seven grams in front of me. He then put the marijuana into a sandwich baggy and handed it to me. "Let me smoke you up before you bail, man. It's been too long to just grab 'n go!"

"Twist my arm, mother fucker," I laughed.

"I totally insist, man. It's been a minute," Ronny said as we went back into the living room where he offered me a drink. "You wanna beer?"

"No thanks. I'll just have a glass of water, if that's alright?" I asked as I took a seat at the far right hand side of the sofa.

"No, that's not alright! Who the fuck drinks water?" Ronny joked.

"Never acquired the taste for beer? And you call yourself a man!" Cross smirked after his attempt to knock me down a peg.

"Just not in the mood at the moment.

I've already had plenty of drinks today."

Cross snorted as he sneered, "Whatever, man. You're just too good for our cheap stuff, huh?"

"Here ya go, Jessie," Ronny said as he handed me a glass of ice water and sat in the middle of the couch, separating Jeremy and me.

"Let's smoke," Cross said to reinforce the idea that we were actually going to get high.

"So, how've you been, Jessie?" Ronny asked.

"I'm okay. Work has been pretty weird," I explained. "Took over a few weeks back after corporate came in and fired our boss. It's been totally crazy ever since."

"Otis said something about them firing your boss. He says you're holding it down just fine, though," Ronny quoted.

Cross chugged the rest of the beer that he had been nursing since I had arrived, "Ah, yeah. That's good. Gonna get me another one."

"Otis say anything else?" I asked.

"He hasn't been talking shit, if that's what you mean," Ronny said casually. "Really, man. He hasn't complained. Says it's a weird environment that's guaranteed to get worse when corporate does get around to replacing the old boss with someone that better reflects their vision or something."

"That's cool. I'm not too worried about Otis venting about work. It's cool if he does. That's the way it goes. No big deal. It's the things that have been happening for a while. Heard you stopped in and talked to Otis about Penelope and the others cooking meth, Jeremy. I've got a question on that whole thing."

"The fuck?" Cross seemed confused.

"The meth lab that Ms. Rice and her two male accomplices had set up in room 329 recently. Otis said that you told him about it. That was our go ahead to call the cops. DEA showed up! You guys hear about this?" I felt excited in an anxious way.

"Yeah, we heard about that shit," Ronny said.

"Yeah. I got into a fight with Penelope," Cross spoke with a seething anger that he had concealed beneath the surface. He appeared calm, but I knew as I felt the same, and he muttered, "That fuckin' bitch."

"Question," I stated.

"Huh?" Cross grunted.

"I saw the two guys getting taken away after the bust. Did Penelope give 'em the slip?" I asked.

Awkward silence washed over the room and created a tension that triggered the sound of scraping metal inside of my head.

"She's been considered a missing person since then," Cross finally said.

"So, she never went to Texas?" I inquired.

They were confused. The scraping metal noise filled the room again until Cross spoke, "She's considered a fugitive, but no one knows where she is. Where the fuck did you hear anything about fucking Texas?"

"We're pretty sure she's dead," Ronny

said as subtly as he could manage.

Jeremy Cross started to cry. I thought it was impossible for him to care about anyone or anything else. For the first time I felt something for Cross other than reactionary negativity. "For real, man. Who said anything about Texas? What do you know?"

"Otis told me that you told him that Penelope got word early about the coming raid and got out of there beforehand. Claimed that you informed him that she escaped to Texas," I confirmed.

"You're lying!" Cross yelled as he wept. "You're lying!" he yelled again as he stood up. "What do you know? You worthless fuck!"

Ronny stood up to stand in between Cross and me as I too got out of my seat and created some space between myself and them. "Chill out, Jeremy. Jessie didn't do anything. Calm down, dude."

"He knows something, and that's enough for me. I'm gonna fuck him up!" Cross shouted in an attempt to intimidate me.

"Ronny, I need to ask you a question now," I said as I balled my hands into fists.

"Sup man?" Ronny replied while staring Jeremy down.

"You wanna suck his dick for defending you?" Cross said.

"Fuck you, Cross. Sit down," I barked.

"Both of you bitches sit down, and we'll sort this out," Ronny ordered.

I sat down in an armchair near the front door while the other two took their seats on the couch.

"I'm not gonna forget this, Wilson," Cross threatened.

"Ask your question, Jessie," Ronny growled.

"I saw what was in your safe," I started, "and I'm not stupid; I know certain specifics about your business."

"Go on," Ronny suggested.

"Did you ever get your hands on that death heroin that's been killing people?" I intently asked.

Silence filled the void until the scraping metal sound returned and overwhelmed before Ronny answered, "Yes."

"What did you do when you found out it was killing people?" I greedily inquired.

"You talk about business. That's what we call a loss. As soon as I caught word that what I was selling was ending lives, I flushed the remaining inventory and contacted those who bought some, fucking told them, and offered refunds. I only lost one friend to it, and in this business that's not too bad."

"Did you sell some to Otis?"

Ronny took his eyes off of Cross for the first time as he looked over at me and with tears in his eyes he said, "I did. Said he'd make a mint at the hotel. When I informed him of what it was, he seemed genuinely surprised, disappointed in the product, and assured me that he'd dispose of it appropriately."

Looking at both of them from across the room, I felt the tension saturate my skin as I confessed, "Somehow I have developed the theory that Otis knew what he had, and has rejoiced in killing guests at the hotel."

"Man, I don't wanna know this. I'm gonna need to smoke some crystal," Cross said, his voice shaking as hard as his brittle branch-like limbs.

"Me too." Ronny's voice now carried a depressed tone as the anger of the moment had passed. He then got up and went to his room to grab the pipe used for smoking meth. It took a couple of minutes for him to prepare their mess.

While Ronny was away and out of earshot, Cross and I established and held eye contact for a couple of seconds before he finally said, "I hope he fucking kills you too."

"You're one of those people who will never change," I bluntly stated.

"Like you've grown as a person," Cross said as his eyes widened.

"I won't argue. You and I are equally pathetic. While you hope Otis will kill me, I figure you'll end up killing yourself. Best of luck, asshole," I said as I walked out of the apartment.

I'm pretty sure I heard Cross blurt out an extra "Fuck you" as I shut the door behind me.

15

Everything settled down at the Blue Moon for about a week after finding those four kids. Moods following the event were quiet and morbidly down. The following day I checked the trunk of the Volvo to find the body was missing and the interior had been cleaned pretty well. Martinez didn't bother to contact me again and literally skipped over me during the conference call the following Monday. Otis and I continued to converse in between shifts as though nothing were taking place. My heart ached at the thought of my friend being responsible for these horrible events.

I had gone from a once a month smoker to a few times a day. The buzz of the pot was nice enough to relax me without being disabling as alcohol usually left me feeling pretty wretched afterward.

Installing the surveillance system was

easier than expected. I placed one camera in the private stairwell approaching the front door and one observing the rooftop garden to cover the possible points of entry. The third camera I set up in my living room as it seemed the most convenient location. Aside from being easy to position, the best things about the cameras were that they were easy to conceal. Had I not set it up myself, I'd have never known Big Brother was watching. Obsessively going over the recorded surveillance material daily from that point, no one had been around except for me up until the night before Christmas.

I wondered about buying another gun. Having to wait five business days to get something as compact as I'd like would be worth it. To be equally armed, as my insignificant pocket knife didn't have any range, was something to be desired. Until Otis directly approached me with violent intent, I had no desire to be assertive and preemptively strike him down in the break room as he clocked in, a reoccurring fantasy of mine that had been developing since my meeting with Von Hertz. I did go to fill out the proper paperwork to purchase a small concealable two shooter pistol. Waiting to be able to pick up the firearm shot my nerves almost as badly as waiting for Otis to break the ice or straight up kill me.

Christmas Eve happened to be mild and gloomy as it lightly rained on and off throughout the day. Windless, the water fell straight down from the sky, and as it periodically relented, a haze came up from the ground in an ominous fashion that made me feel heavy and tired. Working the desk that morning was similar to watching over a ghost town as the only guests or phone calls I received that day were from the handful of people who were living on the property and a singular prostitute.

As the working girl emerged from the fog, I recognized her instantly. An hour before the end of my shift, I felt like turning her away for her own good. It had been about six months since I had last seen Krystal Cox. I had first met her about three years before that. In terms of looks, Krystal was probably the best looking hooker that I had ever seen come through the Blue Moon. She seemed to take to Otis' outgoing personality and talked to him on occasion, more so if she had been drinking. Otis later showed me Krystal's website where she advertised herself in the form of photographs where she wore very little or nothing at all. The home page of the site included a disclaimer that insisted "this is not prostitution, but a professional escort service." The page had since been taken down by the authorities, I assumed, but she was a good egg among prostitutes as she never argued over the rates, dealt with her johns quietly, and was typically off of the property within an hour or two leaving very little to clean up. She lied when we first met, claiming to me that she was not having sex but was in fact, simply dancing while the patron watched. Wolfgang would confirm that condoms in the trash can contradicted her initial story. Did she really think we bought that line?

"How ya doin', sweetie? It's been a while," Krystal said as she entered the lobby carrying a boom box beneath her fake leather jacket to keep it dry. Her low cut shirt was cut so low that her surgically reconstructed breasts were practically falling out. They didn't look right on her as her petite frame wasn't fit to carry breasts of that size. Regardless, both the oversized surgery and the dyed red hair gave this brunette a more marketable appeal, in her opinion, as she has consistently had it red every time I've seen her and consistently brags about her "awesome tits."

"I've been alright. Corporate fired the boss, and I'm in charge until they replace him. Other than that, not a whole lot. How have you been, stranger?" I asked as I looked up her profile on the computer system to begin the process of checking her into a room.

"Living the dream," Krystal smiled as she set cash onto the counter. "So, you run this place? That's awesome! You should hook me up with a discount! Otis still work here?"

"He'll be in for the second shift at three o'clock today. Picked the right day to catch him. He requested to take off Christmas, and I've been able to work it out," I said as I programmed her a room key to 216. "And I would give you a discount, but corporate has put me under the microscope. Sorry about that."

"It's cool. I'll probably stop by and chat with Otis a bit when I'm done. Thank you, sweetie," she said as she grabbed the key and made for the elevator.

The rest of the hour dragged on as I loathed the time between shifts that I'd spend with Otis. He seemed completely normal, while my acting skills were compromising at best.

I watched as Otis pulled into the parking lot. He slowly made his way and parked in the first space that was next to the office. Other than his car, the view of the lot was empty.

"Please tell me it's dead! At least tell me we're not dealing with freaks today," Otis said as he walked in, not stopping for an answer as he made his way to the back. "I just wanna get paid to smoke pot and watch a couple of movies, man. It's Christmas Eve!"

"Eh, Krystal Cox is in 216. Other than her, there's nobody out of the ordinary here."

"Ordinary here means totally fucked up by real world standards. And Cox is here? Haven't seen that whore since it was boiling outside," Otis said as he swiped his time card on the clock.

"That's what I thought. She was here pretty regularly up until June. Thought she retired or moved on to greener pastures."

"Well, you know, gotta dive to the bottom on baby Jesus day!" Otis laughed.

"Yeah..." I tried to laugh but kind of trailed off.

"Jessie, something's bothering you man. What's goin' on?" Otis inquired.

"Nothing, man," I tried to play it off. "Don't care too much for the holidays. Luckily, Elyse is coming over after she has dinner with her family. Wasn't looking forward to hanging out up there for the holidays by myself. I'm fine, man."

Otis pressed his lips together and nodded, "You sure that's all? We're buds, man, come on. You can talk to me."

Sighing heavily I stated, "Since Elyse has come back and we've slept together again, I've noticed some problems," I paused and gestured by pointing to the floor, "down there. Think I need to see a doctor. Not quite sure, but I've got an idea." Figuring something with a little more weight to it would help cover my tracks, I lied through my teeth. "Think she's got a sexually transmitted disease or something."

"Shit, man," Otis started, "told you she was a ho! What are you doing having her over again tonight? Are you even upset?"

"Of course I'm upset about it. At least pretty damn concerned. Figured we'd talk about it and go from there," I explained.

"But I know you, man. Even if she has given you some kind of STD, you're just gonna be passive and let it slide in order to keep her around a little longer. That's your problem, Jessie, you don't stand up for yourself," Otis observed.

"Fuck that! She'll know I'm pissed. Trust me on that one," I returned. "If what I think is going on is actually happening, it's not going to be okay."

Elyse called me at about half past nine that evening to claim she was waiting in the parking lot. I had shot her a text insisting that she let me know when she arrived so that I could let her in through the stairwell on the far end of the building. She knew it was out of the ordinary, but decided to humor me.

"Hey there," I said as I propped and held open the glass door on the backside of the building at the far west end, "come on in."

"What's this all about?" Elyse suspiciously inquired.

Slowly, I drew out my words, "I'll tell you about it later. Let's go smoke some weed."

"Wow. I haven't smoked weed in ages. Sounds good to me," she said as she lowered her guard and came in out of the rain.

We went up to my apartment in a way that avoided the lobby entirely.

"You wanna smoke it out of a pipe? Still got the same glass bowl I had in college," I offered as Elyse sat on the couch.

"Got any papers?" Elyse turned her head as she asked.

"Yeah, you want me to roll a joint?"

"Yes, I do," Elyse smiled.

"Can do. You want something to drink? Bite to eat, maybe?" I said as I went to my bedroom and grabbed the rolling papers from their hiding place in my dresser.

"Too full from dinner to consider eating anything. Least until we smoke and I get the munchies. But I know I'll be thirsty. What'cha got?" Elyse said from the other room as I had already made my way to the kitchen.

"I've got Coke or Mountain Dew, if you

want a soda," I started. "Under 'juice' I have orange, apple, or cranberry. Water too. No alcohol, though."

"Weird. Since when is your liquor cabinet dry?" Elyse lightly laughed.

"I know it. Picked up the pot about a week ago and have been smoking instead of drinking."

"At least you're being less self-destructive," Elyse acknowledged.

"Word. So what are you drinking?"

"Did you just say 'word'? Gimme some OJ."

After delivering the glass of juice, I sat next to Elyse and turned on the television. While doing a quick surfing I found out there was a marathon of *South Park* Christmas specials that would run later than I intended to be awake.

It was shortly after midnight when Elyse and I were in the middle of smoking a second joint when the outline of light appeared at the edges of the curtains.

"Jessie, I think your Christmas tree just lit up," Elyse observed as she was sitting closer to the sliding glass door.

"Must be timed or something," I tried to rationalize it with the hope that it was nothing out of the ordinary.

"You don't sound very sure about that," Elyse pondered as she pulled back one of the curtains to reveal the lights on the Christmas tree that had been left on the red brick walkway were shining brightly. "What's that under the tree? It's too warm to have snowed."

What at first glance appeared to be

slightly smaller than average marble sized white pebbles would lead me to suggest, "Maybe it hailed briefly. Hey, *it's Mr. Hanky's Christmas Classics*! I love this episode."

"I didn't hear anything like hail," Elyse said with her inquiries moving through my attempts to stifle her interest and change the topic. "I'm gonna take a closer look," she announced as she stood up and started the process of unlocking the door.

"Hold up! I'll join you. Not sure what's going on, but I'd rather you stay in here," I said cautiously.

"Jessie, if something is bothering you, you should be able to talk to me about it," she said as she pulled the door open.

I sprang to my feet and followed her out to the tree. Elyse was already on her knees investigating as I approached, "What are they?" I asked as I knelt down to see for myself.

"Holy shit," was all Elyse said as she dropped the singular piece that she had been observing back to the ground. With widened and fearful eyes she stood up, went back inside, and sat on the couch to make it easier to get her shoes on. "I think I'm gonna go home. No offense, Jessie, but something's going on, and I just don't feel safe staying here. You understand?"

At this distance it was clear to see that what I had hoped was hail was a near full set of adult teeth scattered beneath the glowing tree. A slight shade of yellow was easier to see up close as I noticed that the occasional tooth carried the bronze shimmer of old cavity fillings.

As soon as I knew what I was looking at, I muttered the name, "Bobo."

Elyse had overheard me, "What? Don't mumble, Jessie. If you know what's going on, I wanna know!"

"One of our regulars was a prostitute by the name of Sylvia Bobo. I read in an article that she was recently murdered, strangled, to specify. The article made mention that her teeth had been removed. Fuck, I hope it happened after she was dead," I explained as I examined one of the teeth up close.

"You're serious. You're fucking serious?" Elyse's voice grew louder. "So, why are her teeth here? What are her teeth doing scattered on your rooftop patio?"

"I'm being fucked with," I started. "Someone at the hotel has been murdering select guests one way or another."

"Any idea who? Better yet, you call the police?" Elyse spoke with an intensity in her eyes that demanded answers as she put her jacket on.

"Haven't called the police," I admitted. "Pretty sure it's Otis. I've got enough to know it and can prove that crimes are being committed."

"You've got proof other than this set of teeth?" Elyse inquired.

"I've got a couple pictures of fingers that were left on my doorstep a while back."

"The fuck, Jessie! Why haven't you reported any of this to the police?"

Overwhelmed, I gave the only answer that made any sense in saying, "I don't know."

Anger glazed over Elyse's eyes as she said, "That's a bullshit excuse, and it's not good enough. Grab your gun and walk me to my car, please."

"Pretty sure Otis stole my gun, too. That last time you came and commented on the rearrangement of the furniture, that was Otis. I didn't move a damn thing. I acted like I had done it to not frighten you. My gun has been missing since then."

"Really? Forget it then. Fuck this, I'm out," Elyse said as she left my apartment. I tried to accompany her to the parking lot, but as I caught up to her in the stairwell she stopped, aimed a handheld can of pepper spray at me, and suggested that I "back the fuck off," which I respected as I turned back and watched from a window at the end of the building as Elyse made it out to her car and drove away into the darkness of that bleak early Christmas morning.

Returning to the teeth, I first took pictures of them scattered beneath the tree. I then collected them in a sandwich baggy and tossed them in the junk drawer in my kitchen.

16

Keep on keeping on. There's not much more one can do. With my back to the wall, the only option of which I was aware involved reporting Otis to the authorities. This option was in considerably poor taste as throwing him under the bus with the story I've got would result in throwing myself with him. Photographs of fingers could be traced back to November, and appropriate consequences would follow. A baggy filled with teeth is too great a straw to break the camel's back as my shamble of a life would collapse beneath it. I've already come to accept that there would be no positive outcome for me as my inaction has directly assisted in taking more lives, but I selfishly thought of myself and my personal freedom.

What is freedom? I've been a rebellious teenager who did his share of drugs. I've done as I've pleased in my adulthood and have succeeded and failed accordingly. Yet my decisions as of late have deprived others of that freedom. On that note, what is the value of the life of a junkie or prostitute? Many would argue that once your lifestyle has been established on the bottom as these examples, they're already dead. This is not the case for their anxious families waiting for that phone call where they're informed that they've lost someone. This drug addict who was all but lost to society was held dearly in the hearts of those that had at one time shared the same blood. Depending on how the family deals with such news, the loss could crush their spirits or even lift a burden. It was not my place to be making these judgments. What I had said to Adam was right; I was the Cowardly Lion.

Checking the surveillance footage from Christmas Eve, there wasn't any action. The lights on the tree simply turned on at twelve minutes past twelve. No silhouetted figure ever came into view, and no matter how far back in the footage I delved, there was nothing to be found.

Christmas day was uneventful at the front desk, a day to sit and brood over teeth that had once gnashed in the owner's final fighting moments had been broken and scattered under the tree that had also been abandoned on the roof. At the end of my personal count, only twenty-one teeth were collected. How many teeth were initially missing from Bobo's mouth and how many Otis likely kept for himself was difficult to measure as I only found one front tooth from the upper set, while I remember her having both of those.

Samantha worked the second shift on Christmas. She seemed concerned as her thick brown hair curled in its freedom. Expressing that since Ramadan had ended, her husband had been visiting family in Afghanistan, and she had been taking it easy since his departure, "It's been so nice letting my hair down!" Samantha also expressed fear in saying, "We need to talk about Otis."

Hoping this was over business practices I asked, "What about Otis?"

"Jessie, I'm not stupid. You're not the only one who knows what he has been up to," Samantha answered.

Exhaling as hard as I could though my nose to relieve the pressure in my head I replied, "I'm working on it."

"That's not really enough to convince me. I mean, I know he's been selling heroin. His drugs killed those four kids last week. I'm not entirely sure, but I think he also sold to that girl you found in 113," Samantha stated.

"I had a feeling," I responded.

Samantha continued, "I don't feel safe working here. These conditions are fucked up! This is the kind of thing that'll bring down the business, or worse, bring violence here for whatever drama can be associated with dealing hard drugs."

"I've been considering my options," I nodded. "You'll never be alone with him as I'll be here to be sure of that. Until I have something more than word of mouth, I have no solid ground. I've been watching the security cameras to see Otis' every shift," I lied, "to which I've seen nothing."

"You can either do something about it," Samantha purposed, "or I'm calling the police and HR on my next shift."

"Again, I'm working on it. I'll see what I can do," I said.

"You still giving me the vacation time I requested?" Samantha suddenly changed the subject but kept the serious tone in her voice.

"Yeah, I've got the new schedule up in the back. Check it out. After tonight, you're covered until the thirty-first," I said. "I can work some desk shifts, and I was finally able to talk Abdul into covering a couple of them," I said with my voice shaking.

"Appreciate it," Samantha said dryly.

The day after Christmas I went out to pick up my Heizer Defense Double Tap two shooter pistol, which I kept loaded and on my person in every waking moment. I continued to fantasize about using it. After making the purchase, I loaded it in my car and felt no more prepared to defend myself as I had when armed only with a pocket knife.

My thought process began to change as murdering Otis seemed to become the option that I was considering more and more. The only other option was to wait. To wait until he had me cornered became less appealing than just shooting him at point blank in the lobby or break room area.

Returning to the hotel, I went in through the main lobby while Otis was working.

"You like those teeth I left under the tree? Figured you'd of at least brought it up by now," Otis said casually to break the ice as I entered the lobby. It was difficult for me to comprehend that he had revealed himself as I returned to the hotel for the first time since purchasing the gun. It rested in my leather jacket's pocket, loaded and ready.

Anxiously, I recoiled from the desk and responded, "I've known what you've been doing now for a little bit."

Otis smiled as his body language expressed a certain amount of pride, "What? You wanna talk about it or something?"

"Why? That's it, really. Just, why?" I asked as I gripped the two shooter, "And how?"

"Vigilante justice, man. Everyone here has openly talked about it at one time or another. Even you've expressed the desire to get rid of the trash that comes through here. I'm just doing what you won't. This is me doing us all a favor."

"So killing a prostitute to whom you've been selling rooms under the table somehow makes this a better place to work? Killing a drug addict somehow makes this world a better place to live?"

"To whom we've been selling rooms under the table," Otis corrected me. "Bobo's fate has been a long time coming. I figured you could make a necklace with her teeth. A little something to remind you of all the work I've been doing to clean up around here. Isn't it about time we stopped putting up with hookers and junkies on a daily basis?" Otis said in a tone that revealed his pride.

"How did you get the teeth up there?" I asked.

"It's pretty fucking easy to see you've planted cameras on your property. It's even easier to edit the footage and fill in the time with more empty space." Otis explained. "Since you talk to yourself like a crazy person, I'm also aware that you purchased a little two shooter. Editing your footage was just a first step to the whole process; sending myself a live feed was another manipulative tactic that I've used to my benefit, man."

"Some of the other employees have brought it to my attention that you're also selling the heroin that killed those kids. It was also revealed to me that you gave some of it to Von Hertz to throw me off and buy you some time."

"So, Von Hertz threw me under the bus? Makes sense, I guess," Otis shrugged at the news.

"Your coworkers are scared to come to work," I said.

"You think I don't know that? Now, they've got no reason to be afraid. I'm not going to hurt anybody. What's the shitty saying? 'It's always darkest before the dawn.' I'm just working to make this place a little bit brighter. In the meantime, everyone will just have to bear with me on this. I'm almost done." Otis stopped smiling. "Just bear with me, Jessie. What are ya gonna do? You actually have the balls to use that gun? Why ya got your hand in your pocket? Go ahead, big man. Fucking do something."

Hesitation defined my reaction as all I

could do was break eye contact and look to the floor.

"That's what I thought." Otis spoke up again, "Now, go back to your apartment, and spare me your boring life by disassembling your security camera system. I'm pretty sick of watching you jack-off."

Defeated, in silence I went to the elevator. Once on the third floor, I took the stairs to my apartment. I did as I was instructed to do and turned off the surveillance system as it wasn't doing me any favors.

On the twenty-eighth I was informed by the local authorities that Elyse had been declared a missing person, and that I was a person of interest as her family described her as being "upset" after her last encounter with me on Christmas Eve.

"Why was she upset, Mr. Wilson?" Officer Richard Dormanski made his only inquiry. He was around my height, build, and age with short brown hair and a look in his eye that judged me from the beginning.

Distraught, I lied in explaining that we had fought over her returning to school. I expressed that I had been selfish in guilt-tripping her over her plans to return to school after the holidays. "If there's anything I can do to help," I offered, "please let me know."

"We'll be in touch should there be a need," Dormanski said skeptically. "We'll be in touch."

Otis had said that he wouldn't hurt any of the employees, but with Elyse missing, all I could do once the authorities left was quietly weep.

It's all a depressing blur of drinking and trying to escape until it all collapsed on New Year's Eve.

17

It was the last day of the year when I got what I deserved. Having worked the first shift, I went to the Mexican restaurant with Wolfgang afterward to drink myself stupid. Samantha came back to work that evening for her first desk shift since Christmas. She didn't ask about Otis as Wolfgang waited in the lobby for me to clock out and catch a few drinks with him. Looking back, I wish her threat to call the police would've been more than a casual bluff.

Wolfgang and I drank two pitchers of margaritas while eating nachos slathered in melted cheese, jalapeños, and shredded chicken. Consuming the food in a way that felt like I had taken it for granted, I couldn't just enjoy the taste. Driven by alcohol, I consumed with a vigor to my satisfaction, none of which I felt by the time the plate was empty. Even the alcohol was no longer effective at enabling my desired state of apathy.

I was a wreck, and Wolfgang knew it. While he remained oblivious to Otis' activities, he suggested that I get some sleep.

"Mr. President, I have New Year date with sugar momma tonight. Not going to be here much later than seven. You have plans?"

"Probably just gonna sit here a bit longer, have a few more drinks, and then get some sleep. I can't stay out too late. Gotta work the desk at seven tomorrow morning."

Wolfgang's face contorted to show that he disapproved working so early after a night that's supposed to be for partying, "Ew, that's bullshit. You work morning of every holiday this season?"

Looking down at the bar counter, I nodded, "Yeah, that seems to be the norm for me at this job. I'm not too worried about it."

"Something been bothering you, Jessie. What happening?"

"Got some problems with Otis. Not sure how much longer he and I will be working there," I said cautiously as I wasn't sure how to approach the topic.

"What happening?" he shrugged.

"I shouldn't be telling you this, but he's selling drugs to guests," I said.

"Shit," Wolfgang said with widened eyes, "I no say anything, but if he doing that shit, he need fired. Call police if you can prove."

I nodded as I said, "I know."

Wolfgang left to meet up with one of his lady friends while I stayed at the Mexican restaurant and drank for another two hours. With the thought that no leads had been established in finding Elyse, or at least none that I had been informed of, the alcohol was hardly denting my sobriety. I had drank enough to cause the majority of the human race to black out and yet I remember every detail of how it happened.

"What's up, fucker?" a voice asked from behind me at the bar.

Turning around to see Adam, I smiled for the first time since I had seen Elyse. "Not much, man. How's it goin'?"

"Same old shit. I've got about one more month to find a new job before my financial situation falls apart. But I'm not here to talk about that tonight," Adam said in the neon glow of the bar.

"You got any plans to ring in the new year?" I asked as I grabbed a clean glass for Adam and poured him a drink from my remaining margarita pitcher.

"More than likely I'm just going to drink myself to sleep and not really care about the changing of numbers. It's gonna be another shitty year. My plan as of right now is to show up and help you out."

"Help me out with what?"

"Well, the last time we got together you showed me some pictures, and I told you to not contact me. You remember that?"

I nodded.

"I'm contacting you because I know about the teeth beneath the tree. I know about what's being called 'death heroin.' I know Otis is responsible for everything."

Turning away from Adam, I sighed heavily, "I am so fucked."

"Yes, you are," Adam agreed. "I also know about your new gun and that you've dismantled your new audio/video surveillance system because Otis found out and manipulated it to help him."

"Why do you know all of this?"

"Fucker, Otis has been doing this sort of thing for a long time, now," Adam started. "He used to go at a much slower rate, less than one kill every two months. He used to tell me about it. Told him as long as he can get rid of the bodies effectively that I was okay with it. Never had any issues until now," Adam admitted.

"You're kidding me? Please tell me you're lying to my face."

"Nope," Adam sighed, "Otis has kept in contact and has pretty much walked me through your tour of hell. You've got a real inferno brewing over there."

"So, if you're supportive of his activities, why are you here talking to me about it? You setting a trap?" I asked skeptically.

Adam shrugged as he said, "I supported it until he got sloppy. Bringing you into the mix, the way he's gone about it since, the way he's looking to crash, has all been in bad taste. He's looking to bring you down with him."

"What do you suggest?" I asked.

Adam placed an old school pocket tape recorder on the counter and said, "Take this with you. Fresh batteries and a new tape are already there and ready for use."

"Thanks," I said unsure of Adam and his motives.

"You're already fucked in that you're going to do some time in prison. You're guilty by association, at the least, and in on the whole thing at worst. Your passive approach isn't going to do you any favors, Jessie. Otis told me that he's already spoken to you on the matter. Straight up asked you about Bobo's teeth. If you can get him to verbalize his actions and clear you of being directly involved..." Adam paused as he looked for the words, "it's the best position you're going to find yourself in."

Adam promptly left after taking down his margarita in a single drink. I stuck around to eat another round of nachos as I didn't feel like preparing anything at home.

Walking back to the hotel, I was beyond surprised to find that I was able to walk a straight line. I typically don't feel very inebriated until standing up from the bar, but either Adam or the food sobered me up enough to be coherent.

I remember that short walk across the parking lot well. A mild rain fell from the night sky, and while I was slightly irritated by it at the time, I would later recall it with the affection of a hot shower.

When I entered the lobby, the soft light distorted my vision through my wet glasses. After removing them to wipe away the droplets, I came to find the sign communicating that the desk clerk was away and would be back momentarily. Figuring

Samantha was running pillows, or a hairdryer, or something to a room, I decided to cover the desk and wait for her return.

Twenty minutes passed and not a single guest or phone call would emerge to break the silence. I was getting pissed off at the thought of Samantha ditching her post for this long. Even if she went into a room to smoke a blunt and then follow it up with a cigarette to cover the smell, it shouldn't take a solid twenty minutes. Reaching into my pocket, I retrieved my old school flip phone and called her cell. It was about three or four seconds later that I heard her phone vibrate on the office desk. I peered in to see it buzzing next to another run of the mill romance novel that had been left face down to hold her place.

Figuring I'd cover the desk until Samantha got back or Cheryl came in at eleven, I decided to run up to my apartment to douse myself in cologne in an attempt to cover the smell of booze that radiated from me. I put up the 'away' sign to indicate the absence of the desk clerk and took the elevator to the third floor. From there I went and unlocked the door to the stairwell that went to my top floor apartment. The smell of the old hotel is something that haunts me still as olfactory senses best enable the memories that have brought on such crippling defeat.

Upon entering my gloomy apartment, I didn't bother to look around as I took the two steps from the front door to the bathroom. As I instinctively shut the bathroom door behind me, the smell of the old building was replaced with the warm aroma of wet beef jerky. While I ignored the smell at first, I opened the mirror cabinet where I kept my cologne. Once I had shut it and the looking glass was once again directed at me, I noticed that the shower curtain had been kept open, an aspect I rarely overlooked during my morning routines as I typically did not leave them drawn.

Suspicious, I turned around and witnessed the horror of five naked corpses piled on top of each other in my bathtub. On the bottom of the pile, I noticed Samantha's face sticking out with a cut across her throat. A trail of blood went from the wound and spiraled its way into the drain. She must've been killed in the tub as there was no mess on the bathroom floor. Von Hertz was also a notable figure, his cold face exposing a blank expression as he stared at the ceiling, a day or two of stubble, and a single bullet wound in the center of his forehead. The diary that had been found in one of the rooms was placed over the face of a woman who seemed to be bruising all over as she appeared to be in a state of decay that was further along than the others. I think her name was Chelsie. Krystal Cox was there too, her throat bruised with the weight of strangulation. The final body that was on top was Jeremy Cross. Cross had been killed execution style just as Von Hertz, but the patches of skin that were once tattooed had been removed. His glaring eyes were wide open, and even though he was dead, I couldn't shake the feeling that he was still staring me down.

The vile appearance of slick and greasy flesh piled high coupled with the smell of beef jerky forced my body to twist around violently, drop to my knees, and vomit profusely into the toilet. Tears streamed down my face as my stomach wretched, and I again tasted the bitterness of the alcohol I had consumed. I still can't believe I drank that much and was able to walk, let alone think clearly enough to react at all.

Once I was done being sick, I rinsed out my mouth in the sink, hit the 'record' button on the tape recorder in my pocket, gripped the loaded pistol in my jacket, and exited the bathroom.

"Hey there, Jessie," I heard Otis' voice cut casually though the darkness as I entered the living room.

"The fuck are you doing here?" I asked in blindness.

"You gonna hit the switch, or what?"

Flipping the switch to turn on the light that was embedded into the ceiling, shapes and figures came to form as my eyes adjusted to the change. Staring at me with a violent intention in his eyes was Otis. He was standing next to the sliding glass door. With my old Sauer handgun drawn and pointed at me, Otis remained still and ready to fire as I noticed Elyse's lifeless body on the couch between us. Her throat revealed purple bruises that seemed to resemble the shape of hands. I knew instantly that I was looking at the crushing aftermath of strangulation. My apathy was broken.

"Why?" I choked.

"No time to cry just yet, Jessie," Otis
playfully started before his face contorted
with the surfacing of his own emotions. He
then rushed at me, and he screamed, "GET
ON YOUR FUCKING KNEES! HANDS ON
YOUR HEAD! FUCKING NOW!"

Otis had approached me so quickly
that I hadn't followed his commands before
he pressed the barrel of the gun to my
temple and used his free hand to grab my
shoulder as he shoved me down to the floor.

"Just kill me!" I said as my knees hit
the floor. "If you're planning to kill me just
get it over with! Don't fuck with me, man."

Otis was grinding the barrel into my
head as he said, "I'm not gonna kill you
unless you make me. Now, where's the new
fucking gun you just got?"

"Jacket pocket on my right hand side,"
I instructed him.

Otis felt his way into the pocket and
retrieved the gun. Taking it, he backed away
to his original position on the other side of
the couch. "Didn't know whether or not you
were gonna be honest with me! Should've
figured. Like I was sayin', not gonna kill you.
I just felt we needed to talk. That's all."

"I hate you," I growled in submission.

"Hate me? Jessie, we grew up
together. Years of friendship! High school!
You may not be thrilled with this event, but
it had to happen. You like my shirt?" Otis
asked.

I hadn't paid any attention until that
point, but beneath his open zip up hooded
sweatshirt peered the face of forgotten pop

royalty. "So, you went through my drawers and stole my Ashlee Simpson shirt. We should move forward if you're looking to talk about something, I dunno, important!"

"This is important. Details, man." Otis started, "You see, this shirt represented your moment. It's why you didn't go to our high school reunion. What was it you said?"

Puzzled, I hesitated before remembering what excuse I had told Otis as to why I didn't attend, "Yeah, I said that it wouldn't matter to those people. I could cure cancer and AIDS, end world hunger, and bring peace to the Middle East, and they'd still only remember me for doing too many drugs and getting naked a week before graduation."

"That's right." Otis cracked a smile. "That was your moment. A highlight that should've been your wake up call to get clean. Instead, all you did was kick the drugs that made you trip. You struggled all through college. It was the reflection that you saw in the junkies here that finally cleaned you up, am I right?"

I nodded.

"These days you're drinking way too much for anyone to pretend you're sober. Your life has become a joke! Well, this is my moment. My work will be remembered. I'll be bigger than Jack the Ripper or those Columbine shooters!" Otis said, face gleaming with pride as he drew back the blinds to the sliding glass door. "I only felt it was appropriate to dress for the occasion. This will be my moment."

"What's so important about it? You're

just run of the mill. Nothing special about it."
I really wanted him to stop bragging and
just shoot me down.

"Get your ass outside," Otis ordered
as he opened the door to the patio.

Walking slowly, I went along with it
and stepped into the evening rain. Once I
was about three feet out, Otis followed me
and closed the door behind him. I could see
my own breath as I pleaded again for him to
kill me.

"We're in too deep, man. But you.
You're a true friend to me. You've supported
me all along. What started as an occasional
stab at vigilante justice has changed into
something that I genuinely enjoy. You know
how long I've been doing this?"

"How long?" I droned out to play
along.

"A little over two years. I used to just
get one every couple of months. Kill a
prostitute here, a junkie there; it added up
to something that I felt was the purest joy
I've ever known."

"You never felt bad for taking life
away from someone?" I asked.

"We've had this debate in more casual
settings. Sure, I felt a little bad for the first
girl I killed. Taking life was the easy part;
the rush came from removing the body and
hiding it. But I took joy as I became
accustomed to the routine of it. Things have
really picked up recently. Adam was pissed
off when I left one on the property. You
know, the girl you found in 113? Adam
thought I was getting sloppy, but I've
intended for all of this. You ask if I feel bad.

Did you know that Bobo was HIV positive?"
Otis asked gesturing at me with the gun.

"What? I didn't know that," I said
surprised.

"Sylvia Bobo knew it all along. She got
what she deserved, and the community is
better for my services."

"Why Samantha? Why Elyse? They
didn't deserve this!" I cried out, shaking in
the chill of the wind.

Otis shook his head, "Samantha
simply got in the way. I spoke with her
about it, and she threatened to call the
police. As I've said, this is my moment.
Elyse on the other hand, she came here to
use you. I may have known her for a long
time, but that doesn't exempt her from this
place."

Tears spilled over and onto my face as
I pleaded with him, "Just fucking kill me."

"I'm flawed." Otis ignored me.
"Samantha is the example that proves I
have not done a perfect job. Hell, Adam
knew. It's been fucked up from the start.
These mistakes will result in our downfall.
But while these endeavors aren't meant to
last, I have to admit they've been some of
the best moments of my entire life."

"What now?" I cut through the pride
of the silence that followed his previous
statement.

Otis shrugged as he broke eye
contact. Still pointing the gun right into my
face, the depth and darkness of the barrel
seemed infinite as I stared directly into it.
"Jessie," he sighed heavily, "now I'll take the
time to tell you that you're a pussy."

"What?" I threw my hands up in confusion.

"We're in too deep. I personally can't thank you enough for supporting me by looking the other way for as long as you possibly could. Same thing I told you in high school when it came to asking out a girl; you're too passive! I can't remember you ever putting forth the kind of effort to keep the bottom of boots off of your face! You're not assertive enough to benefit society. Shit, Jessie! You're part of this place."

Nodding in agreement, all I could say was, "I know."

Otis started again as he returned to staring me down, "There is much blood on my hands. As respectable men, we shake hands to signify our bond and shared purpose. There is enough evidence to condemn me. Yet this is the highlight of the whole thing for me! Nothing is more satisfying than taking you down for all of this. But you, my friend, get a choice."

"What are you talking about?"

"In my position, I'd hope you'd do the same for me," Otis grimaced. "Your life is not yet ruined, Jessie. You still get to look forward to prison. I, on the other hand, will be free! Damning evidence be damned! I've got a solid plan to get out, never look back, and start anew."

"How do you intend to salvage any kind of freedom?" I asked as though he were an idiot.

"The same way you hope to salvage any better of a man," Otis answered.

"What's that supposed to mean?" I

asked enraged.

Otis smiled and his eyes widened as he took the gun off of me, placed the barrel to his temple, took a puff off of his inhaler, and killed himself without another word. The sound of the shot being fired cracked as thunder simultaneously roared from the sky.

Shocked to what I had witnessed, I stood over Otis' lifeless body for several moments. The rain continued to come down as I peered over him. His lips were curled in a way that seemed to mirror Ashlee Simpson's expression on the t-shirt. Taking notice of the gun, I didn't touch it, but I did understand that Otis had implied I man up and kill myself after him. This weak man retreated to a dry place to call the police and turn himself in.

Before making the phone call I checked to see that the tape recorder appeared to be operating as it should. I stopped it, rewound the tape, and hit 'play' to listen for a sample. Even through the light rain that translated to subtle static, Otis' confession surfaced clearly on the tape. Though it wouldn't be enough to clear my name, I called and waited for the police to arrive without fear.

Epilogue

Officer Dormanski took a sadistic glee in my apprehension as he was the first to respond and arrive at the scene. I imagined a man in his position would be horrified by the violence and the body count, but he and I are much alike in that our jobs have numbed us when we consider the value of life and loss. At least I did not weep as I was taken into custody.

A year was spent waiting for my trial. That year would be counted toward my sentence of seven. My negligence rendered me guilty by association, and no matter how I cooperated from the start of the new year, it was too late to salvage any better of a deal. The tape recorder that Adam had given me had been my saving grace in terms of evidence.

Those first few years of prison all I could consider was whether or not I had made the right choice. Would Otis have considered me to have manned up if I would've picked up my gun and killed myself as well? Was saving my own life in spite of subjecting myself to the societal consequences a lion's way out? After all of the grief Otis caused, why should I live? I struggled with these questions as my dreams seemed to focus on an ominous and angry old friend who haunts me still.

I see Otis in my dreams more than Elyse. In failing her as I did, my guilt would not even grant me the pleasure of visiting her when I slept. Otis, on the other hand, kept a quiet distance as he constantly eyed me down in several different settings and situations, his glare always questioning my motives in ways that I could not consider.

The years came and went; prison is another story for another day.

Upon being released, I was stationed in a halfway house where the system helped me find a job. I would move into a studio apartment six months later on the opposite side of town from where the hotel was located, hoping to disappear from the area where I could be recognized. Never before has the chill of the winter air felt so refreshing.

I'm seeing a therapist now. She wants me to acknowledge that my self-destructive tendencies are not part of a vicious cycle lifestyle, but a relapse enabled by my surroundings. The job at the hotel was not to be used as an excuse for my apathy, but the setting surely didn't help.

I hate my new job, but stocking

shelves at a grocery store is a lot less soul crushing than the day-to-day operations of running a low-end hotel. My therapist says the line of work seems to be heading in the right direction.

What do I want out of life from here? I want to not look the other way when something bad is happening; I want to take personal responsibility for myself and my own actions.

I'm in need of a goal to work towards. With prison behind me and a regained sense of balance, I fear. I fear because I have been here before in that this catastrophe was the second major event in my life that has defined how I so graciously fall. My therapist asked me how many times I fell off of a bike before I got it right. I'm not sure if I'm comfortable comparing drug addiction and homicidal negligence to learning to ride a bicycle.

Questioning my regret, my therapist has also suggested that one who has never felt regret has probably never lived, but that one who holds onto regret is carrying the weight of self-destruction on his shoulders. I need to let go yet remain aware.

To live requires learning. I have learned that the act of forgiveness should never accompany the intension to forget as it undermines the very progress for which one strives.

I've swung through the Third World Cafe to get a hookah and read a couple of times since I've been out. Alem still works there, but he doesn't acknowledge my presence as I was painted as a monster in the media. I'm honestly surprised that I've been left alone by the general public.

When I rest my head at night, I acknowledge that I can only try to believe. My life is not a systematic series of crashing hard into the asphalt of reality. While perfection is a state I will never achieve, these major flaws that I've obtained need not repeat themselves. This is not a vicious cycle as much as it has been the challenges I have faced. Flaws only become circular if I allow them, but I have come through hoping to "salvage any better of a better man," hoping to salvage a life worth living.

About the Author

Justin Bauer has worked in the hospitality industry for four years. He has earned a degree in music from Hocking College and is currently studying English at The Ohio State University. Aside from music and literature, Justin enjoys sports, politics, and cartoons aimed at adults.